MEAGAN VOULO

Professional Student

D1564630

Chapter 1

May 2015

Today was the big day. Elena's heart was beating faster than ever, as she waited for Dr. Carter to call her name. "Heather Beel," Dr. Carter announced. Her gray hair was pulled back in a tight bun just below the top of her ears, in the center of her head. Her blue eyes were sparkling in the sunlight, reflecting the sun right back at the crowd before her. She paused, then proceeded - "Robby Bolor." A tall, broad-shouldered young man stepped up from the stands. His black hair was stark against his pale freckled skin. His skin tone was Irish but his hair was Italian. Robby reached the center of the tent and grabbed his diploma from Dr. Carter eagerly.

Elena was next. Gazing about Yankee Stadium at the tens of thousands of students, family, friends, and faculty all around her, Elena took a deep breath, felt the heat of the summer weigh upon every inch of her body, and prepared to graduate. There was a slight breeze, but it was warm, not refreshing at all. Elena longed for large glass of ice water right now, or a jump in her parents' pool. Well, she thought, when she got home, she could cool down in the pool at her graduation party with her family.

Until then, she would have to put up with the sweat accumulating at the back of her sundress, which thankfully wasn't even

1

visible under the large purple potato sack that was her gown.

"Elena Brooks," Dr. Carter said, in what Elena imagined was a proud voice. Dr. Carter was standing tall, under the purple and white tents behind second base, shielding her from the intense sun that was blinding to the audience. Her voice was raspy, clear that she had just announced the past two thousand names of the graduates. The heads of the department had switched off every two thousand names. There was a total of ten thousand graduates at this ceremony – the arts and sciences department. The medical students would be graduating tomorrow.

Elena caught a glimpse of a squirrel running by the outfield fence. It distracted her for a moment and then Elena's name processed in her mind. It was time for her to step up to the front of the tent. She clicked her heels together in preparation, then set off.

She took one step forward, paused, then continued to walk toward the center tent, carefully stepping on the grassy field before her. It was just a tad too high, inching its way over the top of Elena's feet, which were open in her strappy sandals. Walking across the infield to Dr. Carter, she wondered what she would be doing a week from now, a month from now. What would her future hold? Elena still had no clue. She didn't know what she wanted to do with her life because she had so many interests.

Though she finally decided on majoring in Psychology during her Junior year, she still loved all her subjects, except maybe Cooking, which she avoided at all costs by writing a 20-page paper about the history of tiramisu last semester. But suffice it to say that Elena was the Michelangelo of students – she was adept at nearly everything – and she enjoyed it all too. She took Calculus, European History, Anthropology, and Sociology of

Women, among tons of other subjects. And she got As in every class she took. She shook her head back into reality. It didn't matter what she had done the past five years – what mattered was now, this moment, the culmination of her work.

So, as she extended her right hand to take her diploma, the certificate signifying her success for the past five years at NYU, she pondered her future. And, when the thick parchment hit her palm, she felt a strange emptiness engulf her, as she acknowledged that she hadn't the foggiest idea what to do now that she had graduated college.

But this, Dr. Carter had told Elena last week, was the exciting part. This was the time when she would discover who she is, her strongest ambitions, her wildest dreams. Yet, the tough part for Elena was that she just wanted to learn. And learn and learn and learn. She didn't want to stop going to school and she didn't think any career could demand her attention and engulf her anywhere near as much as school always did.

Nevertheless, Elena smiled as she shook Dr. Carter's hand, looked down at her diploma, and decided that she would find a career about which she was passionate. She smiled the typical graduate smile into the crowd for pictures, waved her arms, loose in the wide purple sleeves of her gown, and walked down the first base line back to her seat in the stadium.

She looked up at the crowd, searching for her mother and father in the sea of people sitting in the audience. She couldn't find them, but she pictured them smiling and clapping politely for her, as well as her fellow graduates. Her mother, Sarah, was most likely snapping pictures as Elena made her way toward home plate and up the steps back to her seat. Elena returned to her seat with her fellow Honors students in the front row and waited for the other graduates to be called.

"Timothy Valdes," Dr. Carter announced.

As Timothy, a short and scrawny boy with glasses, made his way back up the stairs to his seat, Dr. Carter announced the last name – "Susan Whelsh." Now that the honors students were called up, the procession was almost finished.

The applause came to a crescendo as Susan made her way back to the last empty seat in the stadium. They couldn't have fit a single additional person, which was why each graduate was limited to two guests. There had to have been over 50,000 people there today, Elena guessed. She wondered just how many of them she actually knew, as she looked around at so many unfamiliar faces, feeling like a very small fish in an ocean.

Then, when all the graduates had returned to their appropriate positions, Dr. Carter stepped up to the podium to pronounce a final congratulations. Elena wasn't paying close attention to the closing speech, but the next thing she knew, everyone was tossing their caps in the air and Elena's best friend, Jodi was hugging her. "We did it!" Jodi exclaimed, a pile of purple cloth engulfing Elena. She could feel tiny Jodi underneath the gown, but she could barely make out the curls of her golden blonde hair, as there were silver confetti falling from the sky like snow, covering every inch of her best friend's face and head.

-Scene break-

Elena spent the next month applying to jobs on different websites. JobList, CareerTracker, LinkedIn, and more. It was a never-ending search for her next move in life. She came across tons of job descriptions she was interested in – Psychology Professor, recreational therapist, ABA-therapist, marketing analyst, and more. But, nothing felt like the right fit. She applied to all these positions, but she had this nagging feeling that she needed to look for a better suited to her.

4

Undaunted, Elena continued to apply to anything that interested her and waited patiently for a call or email back about
an interview. All that came, however, were rejection letters.
Not enough experience, was a common comment in her emails.
But how could she gain experience without experience? This
seemed like the dreaded, all-too-common Catch-22 for college
graduates – they need to get experience, but the only way to get
experience is to have experience for that position. Elena had
worked throughout college, but not in the field that she studied.
She worked as a cashier at CVS Pharmacy. Since she was 16
years old, the day she got her working permit, she walked to
CVS from her house around the corner and rang up customer
after customer at the register, with a fake smile plastered across
her face.

She learned where all the products in the store were, but she
also learned about some of the regular customers, which did
interest her with her background in psychology. She talked to
Phil, the older man who came in every Saturday and Sunday
for the newspapers; Shari, the young runner who came by for a
Gatorade on her daily jog; John, the young professional who was
always back for some sort of cold remedy for himself and his
wife as they were paranoid about getting sick. Elena had to say,
she enjoyed getting to know everyone at CVS and she learned
a lot about how people behave and think, which she thought
was a very relevant skill, but unfortunately, the jobs she was
applying to now didn't consider a cashier relevant experience,
so it was like she was starting from scratch.

She tried to craft her cover letter in a way that made her
experience at CVS sound meaningful, but whatever way you
sliced it, it was still "just" a cashier job. Elena was applying for
a career now, not merely a job. This wasn't a summer job for a

college student – this was a long-term commitment to a field that she would be working in for seemingly the rest of her life. She needed to be sure she was applying to the right jobs, and she needed to find a way to get her foot in the door with a place where she felt she belonged.

To be honest, Elena didn't work at CVS for the past seven years for nothing. She worked her way up to the head cashier, where she was making well above minimum wage for New York, partly paying for her college education, which wasn't cheap to say the least. Elena's parents were planning on paying for her NYU undergraduate degree – that was the plan at least – until her mom was injured at work and had to take a disability leave. She had been a nurse at a private hospital, and as the head of the house, losing her job put the rest of the family in a tricky situation. Her dad, a long-time writer, was forced to look for longer-term more consistent work. He found a job at a grocery store and worked his way up to the manager for the past five years, but that didn't make anywhere near a nurse's salary. Elena's family was struggling. Her parents were making enough to get by and help Elena out, but Elena was forced to take out the maximum amount of student loans for her education, despite earning a scholarship. She was now in about $150,000 of debt from her undergraduate and graduate education and her student loan payments would be kicking in soon. She had to find a job to pay the bills. And she really wanted to find a career that would allow her to help out her family too.

She started to get worried after the rush of rejection emails and calls rolled in. As the first month out of school was drawing to a close, Elena was getting concerned about finances, despite continuing to work at CVS part-time.

It was five days after her last rejection when she saw the

posting on JobList. She couldn't believe it– Professional Student. It piqued her interest. After reading the description, she knew she had to apply:

NYS Department of Learning (NYSDL) seeks Professional Student. The applicant must hold a Master's degree from an accredited university in New York with at least a 3.9 GPA. The ideal candidate will have an unyielding thirst for knowledge, a way with words, experience teaching, and varying interests...

The description was no doubt a bit vague. It didn't tell Elena exactly what she'd be doing as a Professional Student, but she knew she fit all the criteria.

This is an entry level position, but those with extracurricular activities, volunteer work, and internships will be prioritized

She followed the link to the supplemental information, which included a synopsis of the NYSDL, their mission – to produce great leaders – and their current hiring needs. They looked for ambitious young men and women who would go to school for the next ten years in preparation for a major leadership role, whether that be in government, business, healthcare, science, or another public sector. As Elena's eyes made it to the bottom of the page, a smile crept up her face. She had found her passion! She didn't know how she would get the job yet, but she knew she wanted it and she would do everything in her power to get what she wanted. Her heart leapt.

It felt like her wish had been granted. She'd always loved learning and she wanted a job that would allow her to absorb knowledge about a wide variety of topics; it seemed like she'd basically be a professional student, that is, until she fulfilled her role as a leader. She didn't know what exactly she would want to lead yet, but she had ten years to figure that out. And, at the bottom of the page, it said there was a placement program at the completion of the schooling portion of the position. She would be matched to a leadership position that was best suited for her skillset and passion. Finally, all her schooling would pay off.

Her Master's degree was in Psychology. Elena didn't really know why she picked that major. Honestly, she liked the variety of classes that were required for the degree. That program gave her the most freedom to choose what she wanted to learn. But when the program ended, rather than feeling proud or relieved, she felt empty, basically stuck in her apartment all day with nothing to do but cook or clean — her least favorite activities.

She wanted more. She didn't want the learning to be over. So, she felt that this job posting – the Professional Student – would be the best fit for her. Elana updated her resume and cover letter right away. She looked up best practices for updating these documents for this field and made sure she used all the buzzwords. *Natural leader, intuitive communicator, descriptive writer,* and *lifelong learner.* After she felt that her resume perfectly reflected her experience and knowledge, and her cover letter deftly articulated her passion for the position, she submitted both documents. Then it was time to wait impatiently for the next few days to hear back about the status of her application.

Chapter 2

The next morning, Elana awoke at the crack of dawn and immediately checked her email. She jumped from her bed to her desk and flipped her laptop open before she fully opened her eyes. Two rejection emails, but nothing from the NYSDL. She turned from her desk to her open window and looked outside to see a partly cloudy summer day. The sun was shining bright behind a few clouds and Elena could feel the heat of the season beating into her room and onto her black desk, warming it to the touch.

She got dressed – a simple pair of jeans and a tank top. The green top brought out the emerald tint in her eyes. Her brown wavy hair fell down to the middle of her back, and she swept it into a high bun with a scrunchie to keep it out of the way. She glanced at herself in the mirror – not bad, she thought. Then again, she didn't have a job yet, so she didn't have any reason to get dressed professionally or even care about her appearance at all. She couldn't wait to go shopping for professional clothes. She never had a reason to wear business clothes in the past, except for the few conferences she attended while at NYU, but even then, it was just for one day out of the year for the most part. She was excited to have somewhere to go every morning – a reason to care what she looked like and present herself professionally. That time would come.

She went downstairs to make breakfast – toast, yogurt, and juice – a meal that she could handle. But before she finished her orange juice, just around 10:00, her cell phone rang. She checked the number and didn't recognize it, but she had applied to so many jobs over the past month – it could be anyone on the other end of the line. She hoped that it was a good call, but she also didn't want to set herself up to be disappointed.

"Hello?" Elena answered.

"Hello, can I please speak with Elena Brooks?" said a deep, friendly voice over the phone.

"This is she," Elena responded quickly.

"I'm Mark from the NYSDL and I received your application for the Professional Student position." He paused. "I was astounded by your credentials. Frankly, this is an elite program and we have to go through a rigorous application process to find the right fit, but we'd like you to move on to the next round of interviews. Are you available at all this week, preferably before noon?" he asked confidently.

"However," he continued before she could reply, "I want to make sure you know what you're getting into. You read the job description, correct?" He sounded skeptical. "I mean, not many people want to go to school for another ten years, especially after just graduating from a Master's program," he chuckled.

"Yes, I read the description," she confirmed, as she twirled a strand of her hair that had slipped out of the bun around her finger. "And I have open availability for the next week," Elena said. "I can come in for an interview any day before noon."

"Great," Mark replied, though it sounded like his mind was elsewhere. Elena wondered just how many people he had called today and had the same conversation.

But before she could doubt herself any more than she already did, Mark said, "How about Tuesday at 10 a.m.? Does that work for you?"

"Of course," Elena replied. "Is the address on the website the location for the interview?"

"Yes. But it's room 102B − first floor down the hall to the right. I look forward to meeting you."

"Thank you," Elena said. "I look forward to hearing more about the position." Her fingers were drumming against the table as she waited to hang up and start preparing.

"Have a nice day," Mark said. There was a brief pause, but then Mark said, "I will send you an email invitation. Does the email on your resume work for you?"

"Yes," Elena said. "That's perfect," she added.

"Great," he said in that same bored tone. "Bye." And that was it. He hung up right away and Elena was left wondering how on earth she would prepare for this interview in just two days. She had never gone on a professional interview before, other than the casual interview to get into her Master's program, and she didn't think that really counted − they went out for pizza while she talked to the other grad students in the Psychology department − that hardly qualifies as a professional interview. No, Elena needed to up her game for the Professional Student interview. She was always so ambitious when it came to her academics, so why should this be any different, she thought? *I can do this. I deserve this.* Elena said to herself in what she hoped was a confident voice, if not a strong whisper. She would just have to do her homework. That meant reading about everything she could find online about this program. She needed to know when it started, how many people were selected, the selection criteria, and she absolutely had to read up on the committee that would be interviewing her, including Mark Vladok, the man she spoke to on the phone.

After a little research – well, two hours' worth of research – Elena felt calm. She discovered that the Professional Student program was a new program that started this summer, only about a month ago, and they accepted twenty applicants per month for the first five months, until they reached 100 incumbents. Elena so strongly yearned to be one of the twenty that were admitted in June. The program starts one week after you are admitted. So, if Elena is admitted the first week of June (when they make the decisions), she will begin her training and additional schooling the second week of June. Not much time to prepare, but Elena was always one for the thrill of learning at all times.

Finally, she read, applicants were selected based on a weighted average of their GPA, number of extracurriculars, application essay, and ratings from their letters of recommendation from a professor or employer.

As Elena read through the criteria, she became more assured that this was the right role for her. Her GPA was nearly perfect, a 3.99, she had too many extracurriculars to count – including clubs, sports, and honor societies – her professors loved her, and if she did say so herself, her application essay was flawless. She wrote it yesterday and it was about overcoming an obstacle, specifically, being bullied in high school and how that shaped her into the person she is today. How it made her stronger, more resilient, and confident. She felt that this essay really exemplified who she was as a person and her values – it was a great essay – and she was sure that the committee would love it.

At this point, she'd already applied. She just had to submit her application essay at the interview Tuesday, along with her other supporting documents (i.e., her letters of recommendations). She wondered how long it would take to hear back from the NYSDL after her interview. Would they leave her waiting for weeks before giving her an answer? Would they immediately say yes or no? She had no way of knowing. That's something that bothered Elena – the unknown – being out of control of her fate. After all, she could only do so much to prepare for her interview before it came down to luck. She went through the rest of her day in a daze, thinking about the interview, worrying, wondering what questions Mark would ask her and who else she would meet from the NYSDL.

The next day, Elena sprang out of her bed at exactly 8:00. She made her regular breakfast – cereal and yogurt. She never cooked breakfast; it was a waste of effort. Elena was so excited to go to the NYSDL today for her in-person interview. Never in her wildest dreams did she expect to find the perfect job just one month after graduating from her Master's program. She was nervous, of course, she didn't have the job yet, but she also couldn't wait to get back in a classroom. She picked out a business casual outfit – black slacks, a maroon blouse with a bow on the neckline, and black pumps with a kitten heel – barely an inch. It was just enough to boost her up to 5'5" – just about average height nowadays. She grabbed her black Michael Kors purse, which held a notepad, her wallet, and a few pens. She shoved her iPhone into the right pocket of her slacks. It was sticking out a little on the side, which she didn't think looked professional, so she removed it from the pocket and instead placed it in the front pouch of her purse for easy access. She didn't want to appear to be one of those millennials who are attached to their phones at all times, but she did want to make sure she was conscious of the time. When she researched the professional student interview process, she found that the interview questions were timed to last almost exactly two minutes for each response. Elena wanted to make sure she could fully answer the questions in that time, so she had a timer set on her phone. She figured she could lay the phone on her lap and glance down at the time while she thought through her answers.

Then again, this was all based on the research she did online. Maybe this wasn't even the process anymore. Maybe they had all those instructions about exact timing as a way to test people's nerves. Well, Elena thought, they're definitely testing my nerves! I want to make sure my answers are timed perfectly. She was getting stuck in her head. So, instead of continuing to ruminate about the interview process, she decided to leave a few minutes early and have some extra time to find the facility and park.

Elena looked in the bathroom mirror one last time, flattened her hair with her hands, tucked a piece behind her ear and grabbed her glasses from the end table in the living room. She didn't want to wear contacts today because she didn't want anything to go wrong. No, she thought, what if the contacts acted up and her eyes got all itchy during the interview. Better to rely on her trusty glasses to get her through her big day. They made her look almost her age too. Elena looked very young for twenty-three. She still got carded at every bar she went to. She was self-conscious about that. She felt like she looked like a little kid sometimes, especially compared to her best friend Jodi, but with her glasses, Elena probably added two years to her age. Now she probably looked twenty-one, to her usual nineteen.

She wiped off the lenses on her blouse, put them back on and

14

straightened them. *Right*, she thought. *I'm ready.*

Elena threw her purse over her shoulder, grabbed her keys from the dish against the wall opposite the door, and clicked her car key once to unlock her black Hyundai Sonata. She rushed out the door, though she knew she would be arriving with plenty of time to spare, got settled in the car and turned on Pandora. She had a good station picked out featuring the Goo Goo Dolls and Hootie and the Blowfish – her two favorite bands. As Hold On played throughout the car, Elena rolled down the windows, deciding that she didn't need the air conditioning on in the car today, and pulled out of the long driveway in front of 3 Knoll Court, her parents' home in Smithtown, New York. As she drove through the suburbs, she made her way past the local pharmacy, at least three different coffee shops, the library, and the local middle school. She turned onto the highway and sped through the next three towns over toward Huntington, where her interview would take place. It was a straight drive down Rt. 347 and Jericho Turnpike – fairly uneventful. There was no traffic – she checked Waze in advance as she was worried that there might be an accident or construction work on a Tuesday morning, but she needn't have worried. She hit every green light and as she turned onto Walden Lane, she saw the imposing government building come into view.

The NYSDL office was in a large government complex on Walden Lane. Elena followed the signs to park and made her way to the end of the parking lot, as far away as possible – she liked to walk. The obtrusive brick building was placed right in the center of a wooded area that looked like a preserve. It was oddly positioned, as if someone had dropped the building in the middle of a park and then dug out a parking lot all around it. It was part of the Huntington Town Complex, on the outskirts of town. Elena wasn't sure what park was surrounding the building, but she knew it was beautiful. There were large oak trees spanning the freshly mowed lawn and a bird bath placed in the center of the field with a few robins splashing about in the water. Elena opened her car door, stepped outside, and breathed in the fresh smell of summer. She walked up to the front entrance and followed Mark's directions to the NYSDL office "102B – first floor down the hall to the right" she recited to herself. There was no way she would forget where to go.

When Elena arrived at the NYSDL office, Mark was there to greet her. Elena didn't know who she expected to see, but Mark's appearance was different from what she'd imagined. She had pictured a tall, dark, older man – someone who was all business. But that was not Mark Vladok. Mark was young, maybe in his early 30s, short and skinny, with light hair, a mustache, and large black glasses. He looked like he was ready to lead a meeting, with his clipboard in one hand and a cup of coffee in the other, but Elena also noticed he looked a bit flustered, as he spilt a bit of coffee. He nodded Elena's way, as his hands were full and motioned for her to follow him into the small conference room behind him.

When Elena sat down on the cushioned office chair across from Mark, the nerves started to set in. She clasped her hands in her lap to stop them from shaking, and focused on the notepad and pen that she took from her purse and placed on the table in front of her.

"We're just waiting for Hal," Mark said. "He's the head of the Professional Student Program," he added before Elena had the chance to wonder.

"Ah...There he is now," said Mark as the door creaked open just enough for the tall and stocky man, who must be Hal, to squeeze through.

"Hi there, I'm Hal," he greeted Elena, his hand outstretched ready to shake.

Elena stood up from her seat and firmly shook Hal's hand. "Nice to meet you," she said.

"Well, let's get started," Hal said with a flawless smile. His dark blue suit was tight around his stomach and his pants were just a tad short – Elena could see the edge of his black socks sticking out over the top of his loafers. Elena felt her nerves start to edge away as Hal and Mark looked down over their clipboards. *I deserve to be here,* she thought. *I was meant for this job.*

The questions were fairly standard. It seemed that Mark would be taking the lead. Hal sat beside him and nodded every once in a while, his perfect smile pasted across his face the entire time. It seemed like Hal and Mark were keeping Elena to the two minutes per response, but it wasn't down to the second. Once she realized this, she put her phone back in the bottom of her bag to prevent distractions and just focused on delivering the best answers.

Mark asked about her background, her interests, her extracurriculars. But his final question was the all-encompassing one - "You've told us a lot about yourself, Elena. But, why do you think you'd be a good fit for this position?" Mark asked. "What sets you apart from the hundreds of other applicants?"

"To be honest, I don't know too much about the program – there wasn't a lot of information available online – but from what I saw, I think I'd be a particularly good fit because unknowingly, this is what I've been training for the past five years as I studied at NYU."

Hal's left eyebrow rose and Mark's face settled into a curious position, his smile disappearing, but his eyes questioning, waiting for Elena to say more.

So, she continued.

"I've been the perfect student the past five years. I've gotten straight A's, I've done all the extracurriculars, I was inducted into three honor societies – I'm basically the Michelangelo of students. I don't mean to sound pompous, but I know that I'm good at school and I do pride myself on that," she explained.

"So why not continue?"

Elena smiled. "I would love to go to school for another ten years to learn where I fit best in society. I'm ready to continue learning and growing. I really think I have the potential to succeed in this program if you give me the chance."

And then she stopped and waited for a response.

"You're hired," Hal said suddenly.

Mark didn't look surprised. He simply nodded and put his papers and notes back on his clipboard.

"Congratulations," Mark said as he stood up and made his way toward the door. "I'm looking forward to working with you," he said simply.

"I'll have the HR department get you set up with all the paperwork over the next week. That is – if you accept the position."

"I'd like to go over the paperwork," Elena said. "Can I give you my decision after I finish looking it all over – say this Friday?"

"Of course," Hal said, as he ran his fingers through his buzzed grey hair. "I wouldn't expect you to give me an answer immediately," he said. "I'll have Heather send everything over in an email today."

Friday at 10 a.m., Elena got ready to go into the office for her meeting with Mark. The secretary directed her to go down the hallway back to the interview room where she had been less than a week ago.

She sat down, and then Mark walked in with Elena's copy of the employment contract and her employee handbook. He sat back down at his desk and pulled out a thin manila folder with two sheets of paper inside.

"This is your orientation to your first assignment," Mark said with a smile. "You'll be going to Yale to take a few Psychology classes. I figured that would be a good way to get your feet wet since you studied Applied Psychology at your school."

Elena sighed with relief. *This is a great first project*, she thought. She unclasped her hands and began reading the orientation pages.

It was fairly straightforward. The papers included the professor's name and contact information.

Dr. Henrietta Likert

She would be teaching all three classes that Elena was enrolled in.

"She knows all about the Professional Student program," Mark said.

"You'll have to call Dr. Likert to set up an appointment,"

Elena would call Dr. Likert later that day. She returned home to her apartment around 1:00 and the file said that Dr. Likert would be available to speak weekdays 1-3. Elena decided to call, rather than delay the process. Mark had told her the class would start Monday, so she had to get ready.

Dialing the number on her cell phone, Elena felt confident that she'd made the right decision with this job. And when Dr. Likert answered on the first ring and jumped right into the nitty gritty of the courses, Elena felt calm. She breathed steadily and took notes as the professor told her the website to download the syllabi. She would have access to all the student resources, and more, as she was being paid to be there. As Mark explained, she would have weekly meetings with the other Professional Students at the NYSDL office and they would exchange information about the classes, as they continued to undergo leadership training together.

It was a lot of pressure, but Elena was up to the challenge. This was why she had gone to school. This was why she took so many extra classes and studied so hard outside of the classroom – because she loved to learn.

When she hung up with Dr. Likert, Elena smiled. She was genuinely happy, which she didn't think would happen after just graduating school and leaving her friends and professors behind. Now she had a new school ahead of her – Yale – and she couldn't wait to start her first assignment, and at an Ivy League school no less! Monday couldn't come soon enough.

Chapter 3

Over the weekend, Mark would help Elena find an Air BnB to stay in near Yale, since she would be staying there for the remainder of the summer semester. Mark was extremely helpful and approachable. When Elena explained that she had never lived on her own, Mark gave her a sample budgeting spreadsheet and links to local apartments. Moving expenses would be allotted for moving each semester as Elena's classes changed, so she didn't have to worry about that. For this semester, Mark had suggested she find a long-term Air BnB so that she doesn't feel tied to the location immediately – she can figure out what she's looking for. There would be a decent amount of travelling involved in Elena's job because every weekend she would have to travel back to New York for her leadership and networking training sessions. Elena looked at countless listings on Apartments.com and Air BnB before she narrowed down her options. She was between two places – one was a one-bedroom, small and quaint and newly renovated, and the other was a spacious two-bedroom but it was older. Elena always had her own room as an only child, but her mom and dad were very involved with her life – they were always coming in her room or calling her to other areas of the house to help with chores – so she opted for the more spacious apartment. She didn't really need two bedrooms, but she liked the idea of having an extra room as an office.

Sunday was the big move-in day. Mark called Elena Sunday morning to make sure she had everything she needed to move in. He even offered to stop by the apartment later in the day to ensure that everything went smoothly, but Elena told him not to worry – she wanted some time to enjoy the place by herself anyway. She didn't anticipate anything going wrong, though she had never lived in her own apartment before – she had always lived with roommates in college. Oh, how she missed her best friend Jodi right now. But Jodi had promised to Facetime with Elena tonight to get a virtual tour of her new apartment. Jodi was just as excited about Elena's career as Elena was herself. Jodi had found a position as an adjunct professor at NYU upon graduation, so she remained at their alma mater that summer. Jodi taught in the mathematics department. Elena couldn't wait to hear about her first class as a professor – NYU started on classes last Wednesday. Elena was starting her classes tomorrow.

As she worked through her boxes of things to unpack, Elena sorted items into piles depending on where she wanted to place them in the apartment. She was sitting on the wood floor of the living room now. The apartment was fully furnished so there was a black futon pushed up against the back wall and a large 60-inch TV mounted across from it. The entertainment center under the television held the cable box, a DVD player, an X-Box, and some of Elena's books that she brought with her, her own personal touch. Everything was so clean. The floor was sparkling mahogany, streaked with light stains that gave it a worn in look, but not a scratch to be seen. She had a few piles around her now – clothes, kitchenware, toiletries, and miscellaneous hobbies, like her crocheting, her scooter, and a rather large pile of books that would be added to Elena's TBR list immediately.

The boxes in front of Elena were nearly empty. She pushed a couple of them to the side of the living room to get them out of the way and condensed her remaining items into one medium-sized cardboard box that she figured she would sort out later. For now, she wanted to get some of the clutter moved out of the living room. She dashed to the kitchen, arms full of pots, pans, and utensils. She dropped a handful of forks on the floor and left them clattering on the tile as she put away the other items. The pots and pans went in the cabinet next to the oven. The utensils were places in the drawer to the left of the sink. Her Keurig was already set up in the far left corner, with two bags of coffee out on the marble counter, ready to be brewed.

The host had left a note on the fridge telling Elena where everything was in the building, as well as how to contact the host, and a smiley face at the bottom with the words, "Enjoy your stay!" Elena thought it was a nice personal touch. She felt at home already. She knew her mom and dad would love this apartment, but they weren't coming to visit until later in the semester.

Elena smiled as she folded the host's note back up and put it on the marble countertop in the large, homey kitchen. She looked up at the clock on the stove and saw that it was noon. She would think about going food shopping soon so that she could make lunch – or maybe she'd just order in, considering how much she hated cooking. She decided to revisit the idea of food shopping later in the evening after she got settled.

She walked through the other rooms of the apartment – there

was a master bedroom, a small room which she would use for an office, the living room, and two bathrooms. She figured she wouldn't need to use the kitchen much, at least not for cooking. She was glad to see there was a microwave mounted above the stove – that would be her appliance of choice. Now she just had to unpack her clothes and get her bedroom set up before the end of the day so that she'd be ready for Yale the next morning. Her first class would start promptly at 10 a.m. and was expected to end by 11:20. This class took place Mondays, Wednesdays, and Fridays. The other two classes were 10am–12 p.m. Tuesday and Thursday.

All afternoon, Elena focused on unpacking her things in her bedroom, hanging her clothes in her closet, folding other clothes to put in her dresser, arranging her books and other nick knacks. She also made a list of anything else she thought she needed to pick up from the local store. By the time she'd unpacked her clothes into the dresser and her closet, set up her toiletries in the master bathroom, and looked around the rest of the apartment, her list of things was quite short. The apartment already had all the cleaning supplies she needed, towels, sheets, blankets. The TV was set up with cable and Netflix. The only things she needed were the few food items she would be using to make breakfast and lunch, as well as a few snacks. Mark had told her she had an allowance to go out to dinner each night if she wished, and being the terrible cook that she was, Elena jumped at the opportunity to have someone else make her dinner each night.

Before she knew it, it was 5 p.m. – where had the time gone? But she wasn't worried. Now was the perfect time to go to Stop & Shop. She looked over at the remains of her Chinese takeout she'd ordered for lunch a couple of hours ago, sitting forgotten on the coffee table in the living room. She figured she could eat some of the leftovers before she went shopping, to hold her over until she got back. Sesame chicken with broccoli was definitely one of her favorites, so she was glad she got a large order for lunch, which left enough for an afternoon snack as well.

After she gobbled up the remains of the chicken, vegetables, and fried rice, she threw out the empty containers and bags, wiped down the coffee table where she had been eating and turned off her Netflix show that had been on in the background. Elena then walked to her bedroom and grabbed her purse from the armchair in the corner of the room, with her wallet, and found her grocery list that she'd hung up on the fridge earlier. She was ready to go shopping.

Elena had always been in charge of the grocery shopping when she lived with Jodi at NYU, so this chore wasn't new to her. She planned on being in and out of the store in under an hour.

Elena pulled on her denim jacket. It was a warm summer day, so her shorts and t-shirt were appropriate, but she knew Stop & Shop would be chilly. She contemplated changing into sweatpants just to be safe, but she decided against it. She was planning to spend time outside exploring New Haven, so the jacket would be enough.

The Stop & Shop run was short. She was in and out in 20 minutes, grabbing fruit, vegetables, the makings for PB&J sandwiches, cereal and yogurt for her breakfast. After she got the essentials, she moved on to snacks – she decided on trail mix, granola bars, cookies, and chips and salsa. As she pulled out her ScanIt for the last of the items, Elena's phone rang. Mark's name came up on the screen, so Elena picked it up while she wheeled her way over to the checkout line.

"Hey, Mark," Elena greeted him.

"How are you settling in, Elena? Anything else you need?" he asked.

"I'm all unpacked and I'm just finishing up some food shopping now. Other than that, I'm all ready for tomorrow," she said. "I think I'll spend tonight exploring the town – the weather is perfect."

"Wonderful!" Mark exclaimed. "Well, I just wanted to wish you luck on your first day. And also, I'm going to send over the information about your Leadership and networking orientation. That takes place next week. You should be settled in your class by then."

"Perfect," Elena said, truthfully. "I can't wait to get started."

As she hung up the phone, Elena made her way to the register to the self-checkout. Her total was $76.32 – not too bad she thought. Now that she had enough food to hold her over for the first week or so of classes, it was time to take a look around New Haven.

Elena had never been to Yale before, though one of her old friends from Smithtown High School did attend the school. Elena never visited her though. They'd lost touch after they parted ways for their respective colleges. Sara was nice enough – she and Elena got along well throughout middle school and high school. They were in all the same advanced classes – AP English, AP Calculus, AP Chemistry – and they hung out with the same crowd. But they were always more of acquaintances than true friends. Sara was great for studying and going to the movies, but when Elena was having a hard time in high school with some of the other kids, Sara was not by her side – she was quick to leave Elena alone when Keith and his friends started picking on her. As Elena thought back to high school, she felt her chest tighten as she remembered the bad days during her junior year. It was all because she wouldn't let Keith copy off her in AP European History class. Elena had studied for weeks for the first big test of the semester, and as soon as her teacher, Mr. Collins looked away from the class to take a phone call, Keith craned his neck over his desk to get a good look at Elena's test. At first, she wasn't going to say anything. She just covered her paper, but then Keith made it more obvious that he was copying off of her and Mr. Collins couldn't ignore the fact that Keith was closer to Elena's test than his own. Mr. Collins confiscated Keith's test and gave him a zero. Elena didn't directly get him into trouble, but Keith and his friends never forgave her for that and they weren't going to let her make it through the rest of the school year without trouble from them. Keith was suspended from the football team for a week, causing Smithtown HS to lose the first game of the season. After some coaxing, the rest of the school was on the same page as Keith that Elena had been a try-hard and selfish for getting him in trouble. By the end of the school year, the story about what had happened had changed dramatically. Rather than Elena just covering her paper, Keith was telling everyone that Elena raised her hand in class to tell Mr. Collins that he was copying off of her – which obviously wasn't true. But who was going to listen to Elena? She was the smart girl – the goody-two-shoes. It was her word against Keith's and Keith had all his friends on his side. Elena thought she had her friends too, but she was quick to realize that the other students in her classes were only friendly with her when she didn't draw negative attention towards them. As soon as the Keith fiasco started, Elena's 'friends' started to distance themselves from her, turning down invitations to go to the mall or the movies, avoiding her in the cafeteria. Elena felt so alone during that period of high school, and she never thought it would turn around. That is, until she met Jodi.

Jodi moved to Smithtown during her senior year of high school and she and Elena hit it off immediately. Jodi was everything Elena wished she could be – funny, laid-back, friendly, and popular. Everyone wanted to be friends with the new kid – that was the cool thing to do. She had moved there from California, so everyone wanted her hear about life on the West Coast. But Jodi didn't seem drawn to the popular kids at Smithtown HS. Unlike the other pretty girls at the school, Jodi didn't hide behind her golden blonde hair and tall, skinny stature. Instead, she could be found in the library reading in her spare time, quietly transporting herself to different fantasy worlds each day during her lunch period. People wondered why Jodi was so engulfed in her books, and eventually, when they realized she didn't want to be popular or go to all the parties and events, they stopped trying to be her friend. Jodi didn't care. She was happier alone. That is, until she saw Elena reading alone in the library one day. Elena was rereading Harry Potter, for the second time that school year, and the book caught Jodi's eye.

"I've always wanted to read them," Jodi said to Elena as she walked by her table.

"I just have such a long TBR list," she explained. "And Harry Potter seems like a big commitment. I want to do it right – give it my full attention," she said.

"Oh, they're so worth the investment," Elena gushed. "They're my absolute favorite books. It's not like the writing is amazing, but the story just takes me away from this place." She gestured around her.

"You're Elena, right?" Jodi asked.

"Yeah," she said.

28

"I'm Jodi," she said simply and sat down next to Elena at the long wooden table where she had been sitting alone with her stack of Harry Potter books next to her.

"Can I sit here?" she asked, already placing her backpack on the empty seat and pulling out her own book.

Elena smiled the first true smile that she had in a long time, since last year when everything blew up in her face and ruined her junior year.

Since that moment, Jodi and Elena were inseparable. They happened to both apply to NYU early decision and when they both got admitted, they celebrated and planned out their apartment that they would share next year.

Snapping herself back to the present, Elena wandered the streets of New Haven, looking forward to her call with Jodi later that evening. She couldn't wait to show her the new apartment and hear about Jodi's new job too.

The sun was setting over the horizon, and Elena watched as the streetlights started to turn on down Brown Boulevard, where she was making her way toward the sushi restaurant that she ordered food from for dinner. *Tonight would be perfect*, she thought. She would pick up her sushi, grab a bottle of wine, and take it back to her new apartment, where she would relax for the night and talk to her best friend about all the exciting stuff they had coming up. Elena noticed the sign for Okemo and opened the front door. The bell rang, announcing her entry and the woman at the cash register looked up.

"Hi, I have an order for pickup," Elena said.

"Name?" the young woman asked as she looked back down at her phone.

"Elena Brooks."

The woman, who didn't seem overly enthusiastic about her job today, turned toward the kitchen, grabbed a plastic bag that seemed to be full, and handed it to Elena silently. Her large brown eyes avoided Elena's gaze.

Strange, she thought. Rude, even.

But Elena didn't make a big deal of it. Instead, she checked the bag for her three sushi rolls and spring rolls, thanked the woman and walked out of Okemo excitedly.

The Wine Depot was next door and Elena was in and out in ten minutes. She knew exactly what she wanted – just a basic red blend that she always enjoyed.

She made her way back to her car, noticed some bird poop on the windshield and cringed – she had just brought her car for a carwash. But no matter. She could clean that off quickly. Elena hopped in the car, placed her food on the passenger seat and cleaned off the windshield before she plugged the apartment into her phone for directions back for the night.

It was only a ten-minute drive.

Chapter 4

It was 8:30 p.m. on the dot when Elena's cell phone started ringing. She was finishing up her dinner at the coffee table, so she quickly wiped her mouth with a napkin, threw the empty containers to the other side of the table and swiped her phone to begin her Facetime with Jodi.

"Ohmygosh, hi!" Jodi squealed. Her blonde hair was perfectly straight, and it looked like she had highlighted it recently – the streaks of gold were shining in the light of her vanity. Elena was always jealous of Jodi's model-like good looks. She never had trouble getting attention from guys when they were out together. Elena, on the other hand, was always confused for the cute younger sister, with her dimples and shy smile, more like a half-smile really.

"Jodi, it's so good to see you!" Elena said, relieved to see her best friend after the whirlwind of new experiences they'd both recently encountered. Both women smiled and placed their phone leaning against something in front of them to act as a stand for the video. Jodi had her phone leaning against her makeup mirror, while Elena's was pushed up against the binding of the seventh Harry Potter book that she was rereading. It was just like old times. Elena and Jodi, ready to take on this new adult life they were both living, separately yet together just the same.

Elena felt herself relax as she sat back on the velvet couch and curled up with her arms around her legs and her bare feet hanging off the edge of the couch. She watched as Jodi stood up and walked over to her bed and laid down on her stomach, facing the phone. Neither woman felt like she had to impress the other – they were just hanging out like if they were together in the same room.

"So," Jodi prompted, "let's see this new apartment!"

"Oh, yeah," Elena remembered suddenly. "Let me grab this," she said as she got off the couch and picked up the phone, flipping it to show Jodi the room around her. "This," she said, "is the living room."

She walked from one end of the room to the other, holding the phone up to the TV, the shelves that held her books, the loveseat in the corner. The shiny wood floors.

Then she walked toward the bedroom. "And this is my room," she said, walking over to the window across from her bed.

"I love the view!" Jodi commented.

"Yea, the lake is beautiful, right?" Elena said. "The water is so clear and still – it's like looking at a painting."

"Oh, and there's the rest of your books," Jodi laughed as Elena's phone skimmed over the two tall piles of books against the right wall. "You couldn't have just picked the ones on your TBR list to bring with you?"

Elena looked at her friend seriously. "This *is* my 'to be read list.'" Gesturing at the four foot piles, precariously balanced, she giggled her youthful laugh that made her seem even younger than she already looked.

"Fair enough," Jodi conceded with a smirk.

"Anyway.." Elena continued.

She walked into the master bathroom along the left wall of her bedroom. It was fairly small, and though it looked like it hadn't been redone in nearly ten years, it was spotless. Elena did a little spin in front of the mirror over the sink, reflecting her own image with the phone in her left hand.

She skipped out of the bathroom and swung the door shut behind her, continued out of the bedroom and walked toward the kitchen. It was spacious, to say the least. Elena could easily cook for a whole party of people in that kitchen.

"Bet you won't be using that much," Jodi joked.

"You'd bet right," Elena said. "Not planning on getting much cooking done, especially with all the takeout places near me."

"Fair enough," Jodi repeated in the same sarcastic tone.

Elena pointed out the other half bathroom off the side of the kitchen, but didn't bother going inside. "Just another bathroom," Elena said nonchalantly.

"So," she said. "That's pretty much everything."

"Actually," Elena added, "I almost forgot about the extra bedroom."

"I'm going to use it as a study/office," she explained as she walked back toward the front door of the apartment, on the other side of her bedroom. There was a dark wooden desk set up inside, and Elena's Dell laptop was open on top of it, with her notebook placed neatly to the left, a pen ready as well.

There was a green futon pushed up against the other wall. "For lounging," Elena noted as she showed Jodi the futon. "I figured I'll need to take some breaks from all the work with my classes and the leadership training," she said, tinge of nervousness in her voice.

"Jodi?" she asked uncertainly.

"Yeah?"

33

"What if I'm not good at this?" she asked earnestly. "What if they fire me after a week?" she worried.

"Well then," Jodi said calmly. "You'll find another job, and another and another until you find the right fit. That's just the way it works."

Elena was taking in the words of advice.

"No use worrying about 'what ifs'. Focus on what *is* happening," Jodi suggested.

"There's so much going on right now for both of us," Jodi said further. "We have to just go with it and enjoy it." She smiled confidently.

"You always know the right thing to say," Elena acknowledged, sighing.

"I know," Jodi laughed. "That's why I'm here." She smiled sincerely at her friend, hoping that she would find happiness soon. Jodi couldn't stand knowing that Elena was having trouble right now. She only wanted the best for her best friend. It literally pained her to have her friend suffering. But what else could she do?

"Now," Jodi started as Elena sat down on the futon and held out the phone facing herself, "Do you want to hear about my job or not!?" she asked, feigning frustration.

"Of course!" Elena replied with enthusiasm. "Of course, tell me all about your first day!" she gushed.

So Jodi told her all about the first undergraduate calculus class that she taught this past week.

"I was so nervous," she said after telling Elena about the lecture she'd prepared and the recitation portion of the class.

And so, Jodi and Elena talked, and talked, until Elena realized it was nearly midnight.

"I have to get to bed," Elena said suddenly. "Tomorrow's my

first day in the professional student program. It's my first two classes."

The women said their goodbyes, Jodi blew Elena a kiss, and Elena waved like an excited child saying bye to Santa Claus. They both hung up at the same time and Elena got ready for bed. She changed into her athletic shorts and tank top, which she used as pajamas. She then brushed her teeth and turned out the lights in the kitchen, the living room, and the study. Then she locked the front door and made her way into the bedroom. She turned the lamp on that was sitting on her nightstand and turned off the main light. It had been a long, eventful day, but Elena knew this was just the beginning – tomorrow was the big day. Her first real job – her career.

She laid down under the covers and flipped the switch on the lamp. The room was dark, except for the light filtering in from the streetlamps outside, which shone through the window.

Elena hadn't realized just how tired she was, but she must have been, because she was sound asleep within minutes.

Monday morning arrived like a fast approaching train. Elena was anxious for her class to start, impatiently waiting in the classroom at 9:50 a.m. for the 10:00 a.m. start. She talked to Dr. Likert on the phone when she got her assignment, but she didn't yet know what she looked like. She couldn't tell if she was young or old, and when Elena tried to look up a picture of her on the Yale website, she saw that she was an adjunct professor and therefore her picture was not on the faculty page yet. Apparently, Dr. Likert just started teaching at Yale last year. Before that, she had been an addictions psychologist. She was an adjunct professor for the Psychology department for the next five years, with the potential to become a tenured professor.

Elena found herself daydreaming about what ten more years

of school would be like as a professional student. A bit of doubt crept in as she realized she was basically signing up for two more rounds of college. But Elena loved school, and if she had it her way, she would probably never leave. She couldn't wait to see what the leadership portion of the professional student program entailed, because right now she didn't think she had strong leadership skills. Elena was more of a follower than a leader, except when it came to overcoming the bullying she experienced in high school. After she met Jodi and they became close friends, they worked together to advocate for antibullying in schools. Elena led that effort – one of the few times she really took charge.

Other than that, Elena preferred to remain in the background. She enjoyed excelling at her classes, quietly and inconspic-uously. But now, she vowed, that would change. She was turning over a new leaf and it started with her interview for the Professional Student program. In the past, she would never brag about how smart she was or what an all-around good student she proved to be. In the past, Elena wouldn't boast or build herself up, but this was different – she wanted to succeed at this opportunity and that meant doing things differently. She had to advocate for herself and take charge of her future.

So, as she sat in the hard-backed chair pushed up to the long, smooth, black tabletop, she decided that during this Clinical Psychology class, she would allow herself to stand out, rather than just fall into the background.

And as that thought grew stronger, solidifying into a firm belief, Elena noticed the middle-aged woman who bustled through the classroom door towards the front of the room to the podium.

"Hello, class," she greeted the fifteen students sitting before her. "I'm Dr. Likert and I'll be the instructor for this Clinical Psychology course." Dr. Likert didn't smile, and her eyes were severe, as if she had laser vision pointed at each student. Elena knew immediately that Dr. Likert was not someone she would ever want to cross. She could have guessed as much from the phone call – all business and no small talk – but it was that sharp gaze that made her know for sure.

Dr. Likert reached into her bag and retrieved a pile of papers.

"Let's quickly go over the syllabus and then get started," she said as she started walking through the aisles of the tables and placing a syllabus at each student's seat. Her blonde hair was tinged with grey – she clearly didn't dye it – and rather than giving off a carefree air, it told Elena that Dr. Likert liked things a certain way and she would not deviate from her way of doing things.

Dr. Likert tucked a strand of her blonde, grey hair behind her left ear, the rest already pulled back in a clip. Her face had sharp features – like a sculpture – but everything was perfect. She was quite beautiful, Elena could think objectively, and in her prime, she must have been even more good-looking. She was tall and thin, but she had curves outlining her hips and breasts, giving her a slim hourglass shape. In her sleeveless blouse, you could notice her biceps and triceps protruding from her arms – she was cut. Perhaps she was an athlete? Elena wondered.

Elena listened closely as Dr. Likert reviewed the syllabus. Four exams throughout the semester, they were cumulative. One final research paper at the end of the semester on a topic of their choosing. It was all rather straightforward, Elena thought. They would cover five different units – personality disorders, mood disorders, stress and anxiety, schizophrenia, and developmental disorders. Elena had learned about each of these topics at NYU, but this was Yale – the standards were higher. Elena had to be on top of her game, which meant she was trying to tune out the whispering from the students behind her.

"Three p.m. tomorrow," the boy with the dark hair and Harry Potter glasses said.

"Two shadows," the young woman replied, her red hair bright against her black shirt and yoga pants.

Elena wondered what they were talking about. Then she remembered the Shadow trading cards from her days in the fantasy club from NYU. Elena traded them for a while when she was really into reading all the fantasy novels by Ella George, her second favorite author. She wondered if she should try to talk to them. But then again, she's a professional student now – she's not really socializing with the other students in the class. Maybe she would ask Mark about that. Should she socialize? Should she talk to others in the class? Maybe Mark wants her to mingle. She would definitely have to ask. She made a mental note to mention this when she talked to him next.

After Dr. Likert finished reviewing the syllabus, there was about an hour of class left. She immediately began lecturing. Elena could tell she was all business. Dr. Likert barely paused after she put down her copy of the syllabus on the podium. They would start with personality disorders. Dr. Likert dug right into the history of the development of different personality disorders and the DSM criteria. Elena felt herself zone in on the lecture. She was taking notes diligently. This was much more intense than the classes she took at NYU – the information was so in-depth and complicated. Elena had to pay close attention to make sure she didn't miss anything. She started to worry that maybe she wouldn't be successful in this program. For the first time, she felt like she was not at the front of the pack when it came to academics, and she didn't like it. But, she decided she would succeed, and when Elena set her mind to something, she almost always did it. She was determined. So even though she was doubtful right now of her abilities, she stayed focused on the lecture and vowed to give it her all.

The class ended promptly at 11:40. Dr. Likert didn't really give them an indication they were coming to a close. Instead, as the digital clock on her desk flashed the time, she simply packed up her notes, turned off the smartboard and stopped talking. She was just finishing up with the DSM III criteria for personality disorders when she suddenly stopped.

As she walked out of the classroom, she said, "I'll see you all Wednesday for our next class."

And then she was gone. Elena was confused by how abruptly Dr. Likert ended the class, but no one else seemed to think this was out of the ordinary. The other students put away their laptops in their bags, got up from the desk and rushed out of the classroom in a herd.

Elena had an hour before her next class, which was also with Dr. Likert. She would be seeing a lot of her today.

As Elena made her way across campus back to her car – she was going to run to Seven Eleven to grab a snack – her phone rang. It was Mark.

"Hi, Elena," Mark said.

"Hi, Mark. I just finished my first class."

"Perfect!" he said. "I wanted to catch you before your second class to give you a heads up about your leadership and networking training that will start this weekend. Check your email," he said. "I sent the schedule with the orientation materials there, but I wanted to call to make sure you received everything."

Elena navigated to her Gmail on her phone while Mark waited. She had a new email from the NYSDL and as she looked through it she saw that it was a rather large packet of orientation materials. She didn't want to look at it right now though.

She returned to the call.

"I got everything," she told Mark. "It was just one email, right?"

"Correct," he confirmed.

"I'll go through everything when I get back home after my classes today."

"Let me know if you have any questions," Mark said.

Then they both hung up. Elena had been walking as she talked and now, she was at her car. She took a deep breath, trying to calm her nerves over all the materials that she would review later today. She knew this was going to be overwhelming at first, but she hoped that the leadership and networking training would be worthwhile.

The rest of the week flew by in a blur. Elena attended her other psychology classes – clinical psychology and research methods for psychology. She started to get to know Dr. Likert and she liked her a lot. She was a no fuss type of professor. She didn't layer her PowerPoint slides with fluff or go off on a tangent when she was explaining a concept. Everything had a purpose. When she was lecturing, she was hitting the bullet points on each slide in detail, careful not to skip over anything. She rarely misspoke, and when she did, she quickly corrected herself.

"Schizoph–I mean schizoaffective disorder..."

She never wanted to give her students inaccurate information.

So if she didn't know the answer to a question, her standard response was, "I'll look that up and get back to you."

Dr. Likert encouraged students to ask questions, as long as they were on topic, so Elena became one of the outgoing members of the class – asking comprehensive questions about the material that demonstrated her understanding.

"So why does schizophrenia have to have the positive symptoms? What would the syndrome be called if it was all negative symptoms?" Elena asked Dr. Likert one day.

"Well," Dr. Likert began, "there are multiple categories of negative symptoms that one could exhibit, so it would really depend on the specific symptom. But I guess it could fall under a developmental disorder, a speech disorder, or a mood disorder depending on the specific symptom. For instance, slow speech versus depressed mood or flat affect."

Elena nodded as she took notes. "Thank you, Dr. Likert," she said.

After her last class on Friday, Elena was ready for the weekend. Friday evening, she drove back to New York. She would be staying at the Marriot with the other professional students who were there for the leadership and networking event. They didn't host the event at the NYSDL office because they wanted to have different conference rooms for the breakout sessions.

On Saturday morning, Elena awoke in the king-size bed of her hotel room to the blaring alarm on her phone. The opening conference would be starting at 7:30 a.m. in Hall A, downstairs behind the lobby. Elena sat up, wiped the sleep from her eyes and stretched her arms over her head. She smoothed down her unruly hair, feeling the tangles between her fingers, and grabbed her glasses from the nightstand on her right side. Once she put her glasses on, everything became clear and she could see the time on the clock on the other side of the room, 6:32. She hopped out of bed and immediately made her way to the coffee maker in the corner of the room to start up a cup in the Keurig. She needed her cup of coffee to wake up, even though she knew there would be better coffee at the conference breakfast.

They were expected to wear business attire for the entirety of the conference, so after her shower, Elena got dressed in her black pantsuit with a lavender blouse underneath the suit jacket. She pulled her hair back in a rubber band into a loose ponytail and brushed some eyeshadow on – her only touch of makeup – before she grabbed her purse and headed out of the hotel room, key in her hand.

Elena pressed the down button for the elevator and waited patiently for it to arrive. Then it dinged and the door opened before her. She stepped inside and as the doors were closing, she heard someone call, "Hold the door, please!"

Elena stuck her arm out to stop the door and then a young woman stepped inside the elevator wearing a black suit, similar to Elena's, but with a red blouse. The woman's hair was down, framing her face, the dark brown hair sharply contrasting against her pale white skin. Elena noticed she, like herself, was wearing a professional student nametag.

It said Paige Andrews.

"Thanks," Paige said as the doors finally closed. Then she turned to Elena, her light blue eyes sparkling as if she were over-excited. "Hi, I'm Paige."

"I'm Elena."

They shook hands.

"First professional student conference?" Paige asked curiously. "I haven't seen you here before."

"Yeah," Elena said, "I just started this week."

"Ah, a newbie," Paige said jokingly. "Well my first tip for you is to get the coffee outside in the lobby after the conference starts," she said. "They refill it right when the event starts so it's nice and fresh and it tastes way better than the stuff they serve with the breakfast."

"Thanks," Elena said with a smile. "I'll definitely take note of that."

The elevator came to a stop as the light above them shone on the L for Lobby. The doors opened and the two women walked out together, making their way to the lobby with a small crowd of other young professional students.

"Let's grab something to eat," Paige suggested as she pointed at the continental breakfast through the double doors behind the lobby area. After they got their food and Mark stepped up to the podium to test the mic, Paige motioned for Elena to follow her. They went and got the fresh coffee from outside the hall quickly and then came back inside to a room of silence, Mark standing up at the podium ready to start.

"Welcome," Mark said. "To the first Professional Student conference of the summer. And we have some new team members. We're continuing to expand and we hired 10 new Professional Students this semester."

"Let's welcome them all now," Mark announced.

And the applause commenced. Elena smiled and Paige clapped a little louder than the rest of the crowd, sitting next to her and smiling wide. Then a few seconds later the applause stopped. Mark waited at the podium patiently for the last few claps to end, then he began to speak again.

"As a matter of fact, I have a special project for all of you that I'd like to brief you on."

Elena turned to Paige.

"A project? You mean like another class?" she asked.

"Umm..." Paige hesitated. "Not exactly."

"I'm sorry to all the new Professional Students who aren't familiar with the special projects, but it's top-secret until you're hired. This is when we lose most of our new hires, to be honest. Well," he said, "I'll just turn it over to Frank Fulow from the Drug Enforcement Administration (DEA). He can tell you more."

Elena's jaw dropped as a very large man in a black suit, a strong jaw, and a crooked nose walked in from the lobby toward Mark. He was all business and he looked like he had the misfortune of delivering terrible news today.

Chapter 5

"Hello, everyone," Frank said morosely.

"I wish I had good news to bring you all, news of an exciting adventure that will take place inside the classrooms you work in, but unfortunately I come with a warning, and a plea."

Everyone in the audience was silent, hanging on his every word.

"There is criminal activity taking place on college campuses nationwide. Criminal activity related to trading drugs," he said. "I know this is not an uncommon problem in today's society, but this specific situation is severe. There is a ring of drug traders coercing innocent students into trying and then selling drugs across different campuses across the country and young students are ending up in the hospital due to a rise in overdoses."

Elena gasped – she wasn't the only one. But she wondered, how does this affect us?

"I know what you're probably all thinking. What does this have to do with me?" Frank said seriously.

"But we need you. The Professional Student Program needs you to be our eyes and ears at the colleges across the country. We need an inside look at what's going on," Frank explained. "But obviously, you're not required to partake in this operation.

This is completely voluntary. You can continue to take your classes without participating in the DEA mission, but we would love your help.

"If you choose to take part in this mission, you could be helping us save the lives of hundreds of students across the country. This is a serious problem," Frank reiterated, looking out at all the faces before him. "You can sign up with me after the first break for the conference. But basically, we got a tip that there was a specific person leading the drug ring across the country. We don't know where it started, but we know that it definitely started in one specific school and then migrated toward the rest. If you choose to help, you will have weekly check-ins with a coordinator where you will tell them about any irregularities you experience in your classes," Frank continued. "And we are looking for a few coordinators too. If you think you'd be a good fit for this role, you can apply today. In essence, the coordinator will work with the professional students to do weekly check-ins and take any important information to the project managers, Mark and Hal."

Frank went on to explain the statistics related to the drug ring in the schools on the East Coast and how it spread to the West Coast this past February. The sharp increase in overdoses began a year and a half ago, but the DEA was just now getting heavily involved.

After Frank finished his speech, Mark came back up to the podium. He looked grim. "I'm sorry that we had to commence the conference with this news, but this is an urgent project which requires all hands on deck. We don't want to pressure anyone, but if you think you'd be interested in participating in this project, please visit Frank who will be waiting outside the lobby at a table with applications."

Elena turned to Paige. "Is this what this program is really about? The special projects?"

"Yes," Paige said. "They say that's not the primary role for the professional students, but from my understanding, that's where they make their money and that's where the demand is. We get assigned these 'special projects' every semester and that's when new Professional Students are hired. We've been growing so fast," she said. "When I started two years ago, we were mostly doing the classes and leadership training, but they introduced the projects during my second semester here. Granted, I was the first class of Professional Students, so Mark and Hal were learning right alongside me, but the organization has grown immensely in a short period of time," Paige told her.

"Elena," Paige said. "Don't feel pressured to participate. In fact, it might be best if you sit this one out since it's your first semester."

Elena felt a little offended at Paige's insistence. Did she think that Elena wasn't good enough for the program? Did she think she wasn't capable of helping with the DEA? Well, Elena didn't like to be told what to do. At first, she was hesitant about the whole Professional Student program after that speech, but now she felt more determined than ever. She wanted to make a difference. She wanted to effect change. All her life, Elena had been good at school, but that was it. She was the smart one – not the doer. But that would all change now. She had an opportunity to *do* something important, and she wasn't going to pass that up.

"I think I'm going to apply for a coordinator position," Elena told Paige confidently.

"Are you sure?" Paige asked uncomfortably. She clasped and unclasped her hands in her lap. "I feel like that's a big

47

commitment for your first semester. Really, Elena, maybe you should skip this one."

Now Elena was getting annoyed at Paige. "No," she said. "This is what I want to do."

"Well," Paige said. "I know we just met, but I don't want you to do this alone. I'll sign up too," she said hesitantly.

"But not as a coordinator," she added. "Just as an investigator."

"You don't have to do that," Elena told her honestly. "You don't even know me."

"But I want to," Paige insisted. "And that means we're going to do this together...I'll do it. I'll sign up now. Let's go."

The two women walked out of the lobby. Everyone was chattering and Mark was sitting at the side of the room.. Hal had appeared too. He looked forlorn, yet he walked over to Mark and joined a conversation immediately. Elena saw this as she turned back when she stepped out the doorway. She wondered where Hal had come from.

"I'd like to sign up," Paige said to Frank. "I want to help."

Her blue eyes flashed in the light of the room, seriously, determinedly.

"Sure," he said. "Sign up right here...and you?" he asked, gesturing toward Elena.

Elena took a deep breath. "I'd like to be a coordinator."

"Oh," he said, surprised. "Well, I have the application right here," he said, "but I will say, we're only accepting two new coordinators, and you're the tenth person to fill out an application so far. There may be an interview process involved," he cautioned.

"That's ok," Elena said simply. "I'm prepared."

"Well," Frank said, "here's the application. Sorry, it's kind of long," he added. "You don't have to turn it in today."

He smiled at her. "Just by next weekend's conference."

"Perfect," Elena said, as she glanced over the first page. "I'll get started on this after the conference."

The first page was standard – name, address, contact information, etc. But the second and third pages were essay questions – scenarios actually."

What would you do if one of your Professional Students reported illicit activity in their class? (Be specific)

What would you do if you came to realize your Professional Student was not forthcoming about events in the classroom?

What would you do if your Professional Student was failing his/her class?

They were all kind of vague questions. There was a lot of room to expound upon the response, Elena thought. She put the packet in her purse, folded in half, and waited for Paige to finish signing up for the investigator position, before walking back toward the lobby door.

"I'm not so sure about this," Paige told Elena.

"All my life I've been in the background," Elena said. "I've been quietly succeeding at school but not really making any different. Now, that's about to change."

They returned to their seats and waited for Mark to start the next session. Elena could tell that nearly everyone else in the room was used to this sort of announcement. While they gasped at the mention of a drug ring, they didn't seem overly surprised to see Frank there. Elena wondered what she had gotten herself into.

As Elena and Paige sat back down in their seats, Mark and Hal approached.

"Elena, we'd like to give you the orientation with the other new Professional Students," he said. "Though we know it's a little late for that," he added.

"Sure," Elena said as she stood back up from her seat and followed Mark and Hal out of the hall.

"We're going to conference room one," Hal told Elena as they walked out of the double doors that marked the end of the hall and the beginning of the lobby. Then they walked across the lobby to the other side of the hotel and into a small room.

There were nine other men and women in the conference room, sitting at a long rectangular table pushed to the center of the room.

"Take a seat," Mark said, gesturing toward the last empty seat at the table.

Mark and Hal stood side by side at the podium at the front center of the room.

"You all probably know why you're here," he said. "We usually introduce our new Professional Students to the special projects before they get announced, but unfortunately this one couldn't wait any longer."

Elena and the others looked raptly at Mark, eyes wide and jaws slack.

"So now you know," he said frankly. "This is the real job," he said.

"Yes, you can choose to take part in the Professional Student program without participating in the special projects, but most who remain will not. Without these special projects, it's just not enough motivation for most individuals to stay in school for another ten years."

Silence.

Then Elena spoke up. "So how does it work?" she asked earnestly.

"Are there new projects each semester? Do you always look for this type of project involvement? Do you always look for both investigators and coordinators?" she continued.

Mark looked taken aback, as if no one had asked such questions before, though Elena assumed people had to have asked in the past.

"Well," he started. "We hand out new assignments as they come up within the government. We partner with different government agencies to work on problems they're experiencing. For instance, in the past we worked on levels of depression in college students. We provided training for our Professional Students to identify levels of critical depression and flag them to our attention," Mark explained. "Or high levels of academic dishonesty on college campuses," he said. "There were a bunch of students stealing scantrons from professors and selling them to first-years to cheat. There's always a different project."

"Understood," Elena said. "So do most of the people that you hire stay?"

"No," Mark replied honestly. "Unfortunately, we lose about 50% of our new hires to the special projects initiative."

"Yeah..." the woman with the blonde hair and the skirt and blouse said. "I think I'm going to have to pass on this opportunity...Sorry."

She stood up, pushed in her chair and quickly exited the room, not looking back.

"Anyone else?" Mark asked them.

"No? Well this is a brave group," he said.

"Not so brave," the young man with the red hair said. "I want to keep working here, but I don't want to do the special projects."

"Me either," said the woman with the gray blazer and black

dress pants. She looked shaken up by the situation.

"Not a problem," Hal told them. "You are more than welcome to continue working here without participating in the special projects."

The two people who spoke up smiled and relaxed significantly.

"But the others?" Mark asked. "What do you all think?"

"I already got the application to be a coordinator," Elena said.

"Really?" Mark asked surprised. "Even though this is your first semester?"

"Yes," Elena said simply. "I'm ready for this."

"Very well," Hal said complacently. "Anyone else?"

No one else stood up or raised their hand or spoke. Elena was the only one. No one else even wanted to sign up to be an investigator. Elena was shocked. For all these smart students, she would have thought some of them would want to make a difference in the world, to do something meaningful.

I guess they think they're doing something meaningful by just taking the classes, Elena thought. Or maybe they think they'll make a difference when they're officially placed in their leadership role.

Elena didn't pause to wonder any more. She had made her decision.

"You're free to go back to the conference," Mark said sternly

The group of Professional Students walked back to the lobby together.

"Wow, Elena," the red-head man said, "you're brave. I can't believe you weren't turned off by this turn of events."

She waited to hear what else he had to say.

"I mean," he continued, "what did they think they were going to do – trick us into going undercover?"

"Yeah," the woman in the blazer agreed. "This is sketchy," she said. "I didn't want to quit the whole program, but I will say I'm going to be more cautious about this job."

Elena listened to them vent, and she thought to herself, what did I get myself into? She was questioning her decision to sign up as a coordinator, but as she looked down at the papers in her hand, she felt a resolve build up inside her. She wanted to do this. But, she thought, I'm definitely not telling my parents about this.

She was certain they wouldn't approve.

She arrived back at the lobby and entered the doors to the hall, and found Paige sitting in the same seat she'd left her in. Paige waved Elena over, then Paige turned to the man next to her and began to talk. Elena didn't know who he was, but she was sure Paige would introduce her.

"Hi," she said as she approached, "I'm Elena."

"Elena," Paige said, "this is my boyfriend, Patrick. He just got here."

"Oh," Elena said genuinely surprised, "does he work here too?" It seemed like a strange turn of events for the couple to both be working for the same program that isn't really well known.

"Yeah," Paige said. "I just got him involved in the PS program this year. He's new like you, but he didn't have to go to the orientation because he already knew about all the special projects since we've been living together since I started working here."

"Wow," Elena said, "so you guys are serious."

Paige and Patrick chuckled. He smoothed back his strawberry blonde hair away from his eyes. "Yes," they both said.

"We've been together since college," Patrick told Elena, "so three years now."

"Well," Elena said happily, "it's very nice to meet you!"

Patrick turned serious. "So, Paige told me you're getting involved in one of the special projects?"

"Yes," Elena said simply. "I want to make a difference. I want to do something rather than just learn about things in books."

"That makes sense," Patrick said. "But, if Paige is going to be involved in this too, I think maybe I should sign up too – to keep an eye on things." He looked into Paige's eyes, like there was an unspoken understanding.

"Oh," Elena said, uncertain. "You don't trust us to take care of ourselves?" she asked. She shook her head. "Sorry," she said. "I didn't mean for it to come out like that."

"No," Patrick said. "It's ok. I trust you both completely, but I just have a weird feeling about this special project. I think it would be better if all three of us were in this together." What was Patrick thinking about the project? Did he know something Elena didn't? Elena cautiously continued on with the conversation.

"Fair enough," Paige said and shrugged. Elena nodded her agreement.

"Well," Elena said looking down at the schedule for the day, "let's go over to the first breakout session. Looks like it's starting in ten minutes."

Paige, Patrick, and Elena stood up and made their way out of the hall. "I think I'm going to the negotiation session," Elena told the others. "It says it's about being more assertive in negotiation tactics."

"Sounds good to us," Patrick said, looking for Paige's approval.

The three walked together to conference room 1, down the

hall by the fitness center in the hotel. They filed in and saw someone standing up at the podium at the front of the room, ready to start. Everyone else was already seated. Patrick, Elena, and Paige took their seats in the back of the room. Elena was ready to learn something that she could apply directly to her everyday life. It was these soft skills that she was very excited to learn about and practice the most.

There was a white board behind the man at the front of the room, and on the board, it said Assertiveness and Negotiation. The clock struck 12 noon and the man called for their attention. Everyone was silent and the lecture began. Elena looked around at the other twenty Professional Students in the room and thought, I belong here.

* * *

The rest of the conference flew by as a whirlwind of lectures and breakout sessions, new people, home. She said goodbye to Paige and Patrick and got in her car at 5 p.m. on Sunday to drive back to New Haven. She had class in the morning.

She arrived home at 8:00, and since it was still rather early, Elena decided to work on her coordinator application.

There were situational questions on the application.

You uncover a tip about illicit activity in one of the classrooms of the Professional Student you are speaking with. The PS is nervous and doesn't know if he wants to remain in the program. How do you proceed?

Elena thought about this. Why would the PS be nervous? Is the project dangerous? She thought the DEA had everything under control, but maybe there were additional risks she wasn't aware of. Wait, she thought, what if this wasn't all that it seemed to be? Elena had thought this project would make her worth something. It would make her worthy of the praise she'd always received for her intellect, but what if she was wrong. Could she really trust the DEA?

It seemed like they sprang this on them pretty quickly, so how was Elena to trust that this was the true project. How did she know there wouldn't be another twist or turn down the line? How did she know things wouldn't get more dangerous.

But, she trusted Mark. Maybe not Hal – he was a little off – but Mark was so sincere and if this was part of his plan for the PS program, then she believed in it. She shook the doubt away. Then, she returned to the application question. She remembered the negotiation breakout session, where they talked about being persuasive when you want something, but Elena didn't think that was the best tactic here. She didn't want to coerce someone into staying in the program. So instead, she wrote about how she would validate and comfort the PS and as she did so, she would try to get the PS to divulge more information about what he knew of the situation. Elena used the skills from her counseling classes to determine the best way to approach the following situations as well.

This is quite intuitive, she thought. Maybe this *is* the right job for me after all.

Question after question, Elena went with her gut. She just instinctively knew what the answer should be. She felt confident she would be chosen for the coordinator position if this packet was the main selection criteria.

Elena was getting excited as she reached the end of the packet. She wanted to hand this in as soon as possible because she really thought she had a chance at becoming a coordinator for the project. But she would have to wait until next week's networking event, which couldn't come soon enough, in Elena's opinion.

But she had to wonder if there was even more to the PS program. Was the DEA the only curveball they were going to throw at her, or was there more to come? She would tread cautiously ahead, just in case there was more to the story. While uncovering a drug ring seemed like a daunting task already, Elena wasn't so sure that this was the whole story. She decided to keep a journal of everything that went on with the PS program. If she was a coordinator, she would document her sessions with the other PS investigators – if she was an investigator, she would write down everything she saw and heard in the classroom. She couldn't tell anyone else about the DEA project, but if she kept a journal to herself, at least there would be some record of everything just in case something bad happened. She took a deep breath as she realized this was a major fear of hers right now. What if something bad happened to her?

She couldn't really imagine what might happen yet. She didn't know the specifics, but she had watched enough Law and Order episodes to know that sting operations could often go wrong. This was the most dangerous thing she had ever done, and she hadn't even begun the mission yet. She was in for a long semester.

* * *

Chapter 6

As Elena sat through her classes at Yale, she was more aware of her surroundings. Now that she had been briefed on the DEA Project, she was always on the lookout for inconsistent activities inside the classroom. Last weekend, at the conference, all the people who signed up for the DEA project were included in a detailed briefing of the project and what was expected of them. There were about 45 Professional Students involved in the project, including Elena, Paige, and Patrick. Although Elena was still hoping to get selected as a coordinator, she went to the briefing for the investigators because that would be her fallback if she wasn't selected. She couldn't wait until the upcoming conference because Frank would be posting the coordinators at the end of the first day. Elena had to submit her application the night prior. They were due Friday night, the night before the conference begins. Her application was all ready and she was getting nervous about the selection process.

They only had a day to review all the applications and make their decision. That didn't seem like enough time, Elena thought.

But she shook herself back to reality, away from her nerves surrounding the DEA project coordinator position, and back into Dr. Likert's psychopathology class on Wednesday morning.

They were going over personality disorders today and although Elena had a lot of background knowledge on this already, she wanted to somewhat pay attention – however, she was more concerned with the environment now that she knew about the DEA project.

She looked around the classroom and saw the students carefully taking notes as Dr. Likert lectured. Elena didn't notice anything unusual yet, but she would keep an eye out for any unusual activity. So far, the students at Yale seemed to be attentive, hard-working, and organized. They showed up for class each day promptly, ready to learn and at attention. Elena doubted anyone in this class was involved in drugs, but she couldn't rule it out yet she supposed.

If I get chosen for a coordinator position, I can be more involved in the project and really make a difference, she thought to herself as she continued to carefully observe her surroundings, take notes, and look up at Dr. Likert at the front of the room. Dr. Likert was dressed in a very fashionable pantsuit today. It was a little chilly in the classroom because the air conditioner was blasting – though it was very hot outside. Dr. Likert had adjusted to the indoor weather by layering. Her pantsuit was made up of navy dress pants, a sleeveless blouse, with a three-quarter sleeve blazer over it. She also kept a sweater on the back of her chair, in case she got a little cold throughout the lecture. At this time, she was just wearing the blazer – the sweater lay forgotten during this lecture – and she looked comfortable as she stood in the front of the classroom and gestured toward the smartboard as she ran through all her PowerPoint slides related to Narcissistic Personality Disorder. They then proceeded to engage in a mock counseling session – Dr. Likert leading the discussion and the students acting as counselors in training.

Dr. Likert's blazer outlined her hourglass shape, accentuating her narrow hips and shoulders that gave her a nearly perfect stature for her height. As she led the discussion, Elena remained engaged and participated in each section. The slideshow with the counseling notes was up in the background in addition to the notes on Narcissistic Personality Disorder. The discussion was lively, with nearly all the students participating, but it was clear that Elena had the best understanding of the material.

As the class wrapped up, Elena watched Dr. Likert close out the slideshow and put her things away into her purse.

Dr. Likert called Elena over to her before she walked out the door.

"You're good with people. You seem to have good intuition about how to get people to open up and how to help them solve their problems," she told her after a mock counseling session.

Dr. Likert was very impressed with her work. "You might want to consider becoming a lead Psychologist," she said. "For the government, or education, or healthcare – you can really go into that field as a leadership position anywhere."

Elena definitely considered it.

I guess my Psychology degree won't go to waste, she thought.

* * *

When Elena got home Wednesday night, she decided that she would try to cook herself dinner. This would be the first time she would attempt this since living in her apartment – until now she just relied to takeout. But, her mom called her today and started to chastise her about her lack of cooking.

"Really, Elena," her mother scolded, "You have to learn how to cook for yourself! You can't just get takeout every night –

it's not healthy."

Elena groaned, rolled her eyes, though her mother couldn't see as she was on the phone, and readied herself to reply.

"You know what, Mom?" she asked sarcastically. "Maybe I'll cook a gourmet dinner tonight. A four-course meal. And I'll invite over a whole party of people."

"Ha ha," her mom said, annoyed with her daughter's lack of homemaking skills.

"Fine," Elena said seriously. "I don't like to be told I'm bad at something, and I'd appreciate it if you stopped making fun of my terrible cooking skills, so maybe it's time I learned."

"That's what I've been saying for years!" her mother yelled into the phone relieved.

Elena chuckled nervously as she thought about cooking tonight. She was standing in the middle of the kitchen when she was on the call, and now she looked around at the stove and oven, which were hardly used in her apartment. She opened the fridge and saw that she had next to nothing in there. She opened the freezer and noticed that she had tons of frozen dinners. Those were the only things she managed to cook in the past and not destroy.

But, Elena didn't shy away from a challenge. Instead, she went to the library and took out every cookbook she would find. She then took a long trip to Stop & Shop and got everything on her list which she had made based on ten recipes she'd selected from the books. She was determined to get this right.

She started with dinner that night. It was 7:30 by the time she got home from the library and the store with all her ingredients – it would be a late dinner tonight, she decided determinedly.

Unfortunately, everything that could go wrong, did go wrong. First, Elena spent ten minutes chopping onions and they ended up on the floor. Her eyes were tearing and then when she turned around to carry the chopped onions over to the stove, she had to wipe her eyes and dropped the cutting board filled with the finely chopped onions that had taken her twice as long as the directions had recommended. She decided that the recipe would work without onions, since she didn't have any more onions left to chop. Elena did consider the five second rule, but decided against it when she remembered that she hadn't cleaned the floors in a week – cleaning was not one of Elena's strong suits either.

I'm not cut out for this.

Elena tried her best to cook the rest of the chicken fajitas, minus the onions. But then there was smoke everywhere and the loud beeping resonating through the apartment was threatening to disturb the neighbors. She had walked away from the chicken for a few minutes because the directions said that it needed to cook for seven minutes. She didn't see the note about turning down the heat on the stove for the last four minutes. Then she panicked. She took everything off the stove and opened the three windows in the apartment to try to get some of the smoke out. A bead of sweat dripped down Elena's forehead as she was pacing the living room, deciding what else to do.

"There's no other option," she said aloud.

"I have to dump everything. This is hopeless," she whined.

Twenty minutes later, the smoke had cleared out and the burnt chicken and peppers were in the garbage, along with the onions that Elena finally cleaned from the floor.

Elena was curled up on the brown suede couch, her head in her hands, trying to decide what to do. She determined the best course of action was to just order a pizza, take out all the trash and go to bed early, hoping that by tomorrow she would feel a little less awful about her failed attempt at cooking, wondering how her mother would reply when she explained the fiasco. She decided not to worry about that tonight.

By 9:00, Elena was fast asleep.

Friday came and went in the blink of an eye. Before she knew it, Elena was packing up the car again to head back to New York for the next Professional Student Leadership Conference.

She arrived at the Hyatt Regency at 7:30 p.m. The ride was uneventful – no traffic, no accidents. She talked to Jodi for a while.

"So, how's the job treating you?" Jodi asked.

Elena wanted to tell her about the special projects, but she had signed a nondisclosure agreement at the conference last week. She could only share the information with others in her household, as the situation could involve the rest of the house as the project progressed. Since Elena lived alone, she couldn't share the information with anyone.

"It's going well," she told Jodi. "I like my classes – they're super interesting. How's your teaching position going?"

"Oh, it's great," Jodi gushed. "The students really seem to like me and I'm having so much fun planning different activities for all of them during the recitation sections. I do a lot of group work with them…"

Jodi went on to describe her job for the next hour. It was easy for Elena to keep Jodi focused on herself rather than asking about Elena. Dr. Likert was right – Elena had a way with people. Jodi didn't seem to realize that Elena kept turning the conversation back to her every few questions. People liked to talk about themselves, Elena realized – and Jodi was no different.

"There must be something exciting about the Professional Student program," Jodi pushed. "It can't be all nerds like you just taking classes for the rest of their lives," she added with a laugh.

Elena felt bad keeping something this big from her best friend, but what could she do? She didn't feel this badly about lying to her mom – for some reason that was different. She didn't typically lie to her mother, but there were certainly things she left out throughout her childhood, namely the bullying. She never told her mom how much the other students teased her – she was embarrassed, so she kept that information to herself. Elana hadn't wanted to trouble her mom with her problems, and felt similarly now. The DEA project would worry her mom and there was no reason to, in Elena's opinion. Her mom had enough to worry about with all the financial struggles she and Dad were facing. Dad's job was still underpaying him, and Mom's back was still bothering her, getting stiffer and stiffer as she aged.

"It's just the classes," Elena said brightly. "They're really interesting. It is actually very exciting," she told Jodi distractedly. She decided she couldn't tell her too much about the PS program or she'd risk spilling the truth. But, maybe she should tell her. Maybe Jodi had a right to know what was really going on with her. But Elena always followed the rules, and she'd signed a nondisclosure agreement at the conference last week – all the volunteers had. They agreed not to divulge any of the information that they heard in their briefing meeting – and that was basically everything. Elena didn't think there was any way around the rules. Although, Paige had told Patrick all about the past secret operations before he was officially a Professional Student, and they still accepted him into the program, so was it really that bad to tell one person the truth?

Elena realized she was staring ahead, driving on autopilot, not listening to Jodi anymore.

"Elena? Did I lose you?" Jodi asked.

"Nope," Elena said. "Still here." She snapped herself out of her reverie. She couldn't break the rules. She would have to continue to lie. She couldn't risk getting kicked out of the program. She needed this job. Her parents were counting on her to support herself – she couldn't let them down.

So, Elena continued the light conversation with Jodi for another hour, until she got to the Hyatt.

When she arrived at the hotel, she was tired. Her eyes were closing on their own and she was stiff from sitting in the car for the past two and a half hours.

She checked in at the front desk and headed up to her room on the second floor to put her stuff away. She was planning on meeting Paige and Patrick down at the hotel bar later in the evening. She wasn't really in the mood for a drink at the moment, but she figured she would perk up once she got back to her room and made a cup of coffee.

Elena almost forgot, she had to drop off her application with Hal and Mark tonight if she wanted to be considered for the coordinator position. They had instructed her to come to the conference room after 7 p.m. to drop off the application and certify her interest in the position.

After she stopped at her room quickly to make the cup of coffee, she unpacked her things in a hurry and found her application. It was perfectly straight, as if she had just ironed it, though it was just sitting nicely in her purse, and she double-checked everything as she walked out of the room.

Her coffee cup in her hand, taking a sip as she closed the room door behind her, she made her way back towards the lobby and to Conference room 2. She was wearing mid-rise jeans with a black short sleeve shirt, a chunky silver necklace, and black ballet flats. She didn't like to wear sweats even when she was sitting in a long car ride. She always liked to be put together now that she'd started her job as a PS.

The conference room door was propped open when she arrived and Elena saw Frank, Hal, and Mark inside the room talking in hushed tones.

"Yes, we'll have to look into that," Hal said. "I don't know if that's a serious lead."

"We have to check it out though," Mark responded.

Frank looked up at Elena and silenced the other two men.

"Hello," Frank said.

"Hi, Elena," Mark said cheerfully.

"Hi, Mark, Hal, Frank," Elena replied.

"Elena is one of our new PS recruits," Mark explained to Frank. "She was very interested in the DEA project."

"Yes," Elena confirmed. "I actually came to drop off my coordinator application."

"But you're new?" Hal asked in a disdainful tone.

"Yes," Elena said. "I figured this would be a great way for me to get fully immersed in the program," she told them earnestly.

"Well," Hal said, his grey hair glowing in the long light of the conference room, shining above him. "We don't usually accept first-semester PS recruits." He'd said it with dour disinterest. He held out his left hand to take her application, but Elena turned to Mark and handed it to him.

"I appreciate your consideration for this important position," she said to Mark. Then she turned to Frank and Hal. "And I look forward to hearing your decision."

She turned around and walked out of the conference room confidently. She did the best she could and the application was stellar. Now all she could do was wait. She looked down at her phone. 8:02 p.m. She would go back to her room and fix up her makeup before she met Paige and Patrick downstairs at the bar. She wasn't going to stay up too late – they had an early start for the conference tomorrow – 7 a.m. opening ceremony.

Elena expected to hear back about her application by tomorrow evening. They didn't say when exactly they would let the applicants know, but they assured them that the final decision would be made before Sunday, so that the chosen coordinators could undergo their orientation Sunday while the other PS recruits were in their breakout sessions.

After Elena fixed her eyeshadow, she went back down the stairs. She didn't want to take the elevator just to go down one floor. So, as she stepped out of the stairwell, she saw the hotel bar and out of the corner of her eye, Paige's pale face and dark hair.

Elena waved to Paige and then she saw Patrick sitting by Paige's side and acknowledged him with a nod, as she sat down on the barstool on Paige's other side.

"What are you drinking?" Elena asked in the general direction of Paige and Patrick, hoping to get answers from both of them.

"Just a Vodka and Cranberry," Paige said, gesturing at both their drinks. "Want one?" she asked.

"I'll just get a glass of wine," Elena replied and made eye contact with the bartender. He walked over to the group. His blue eyes were electrifying, as if they were lasers going right through Elena, reading her mind.

"A drink for you, Miss?" he asked politely. "I'm Greg by the

67

way. I'll be here all night."

"I'll just have a glass of the house red, please," Elena ordered. "And nice to meet you, Greg."

Greg reached out his hand towards Elena, she shook it and felt how much larger his hand was compared to hers. Elena was tiny compared to Greg – he was about 6 foot 2, whereas Elena was only 5 foot 3 and petite, almost childlike.

She smiled at Greg and he stepped away to pour her drink.

"$6," he said when he returned with the large glass of red wine.

Elena rummaged in her purse for her credit card.

"Do you want to start a tab?" Greg asked.

"No," Elena replied quickly. "I'm just having this one drink, thanks." She slowly took a sip of her wine – fruity and smooth – exactly what she wanted.

Elena turned to Paige and Patrick who were deep in conversation, it seemed.

"I don't know," Paige said to Patrick in a whisper, "she's still fairly new."

Patrick coughed into his hand and looked in Elena's direction.

"Oh, Elena, you got your drink?" Paige asked, flustered.

"Yeah," Elena said. "So, how have you guys been!? I know it's only been a week, but it seems like a lot has happened, what with the application process and school..."

"Yes," Paige said. "It's definitely been a busy week."

"The project has begun," Patrick said casually, "so we're ready to do our part."

"Same," Elena said. "I just can't wait to hear back about my application." She didn't want to say too much in a public place, but she figured she could reference an application with no suspicions.

"Tomorrow," Patrick and Paige said together. Then they giggled. "Jinx," Paige said. "You owe me another drink."

And so they talked for an hour about their week, discussing their classes and trying to learn more about each other since they hadn't talked much last weekend.

"So you're an only child?" Paige asked Elena as she was telling a story about her mom.

"Yes, it's just me and my mom and my dad," Elena said simply.

"Wow!" Paige said. "I can't imagine what growing up in a house as an only child is like. I have five brothers," she said.

"And I have a brother and two sisters," Patrick said. "Although, neither of us are particularly close to our siblings."

Elena talked about school and growing up with her mom before she was injured as a nurse, of all the long hours at the hospital, her dad's career as a writer up until recently, and more.

Elena tried to ask Paige about the PS program and what she's done so far, but Paige and Patrick were elusive about the specifics. This made sense, Elena thought, because all the projects were secret, for the most part. So, Elena steered the conversation away from work. They talked and talked and before they knew it, it was 10:30. Elena looked down at her phone and saw the time.

"Oh," she said. "It's getting kind of late. I think I'm going to turn in for the night. We do have an early morning tomorrow."

"Ok. 'Night," Paige said as she gestured for Greg to bring the bill. Paige and Patrick were a few drinks in. They'd started a tab when they got there. Elena stood up and was ready to head back to her room.

"I've got it," Patrick said, pulling out his wallet from his right pocket.

"Thanks," Paige said.

"Well," Elena said, "I'll see you guys in the morning!"

She waved goodbye and made her way toward the staircase. She yawned as she reached the door of her room and she quickly got changed into her pajamas and into bed. She wanted it to be a fairly early night because she had been up so late working on schoolwork the past week. She needed this weekend to catch up on some sleep.

She set her alarm for 6:30 a.m. and rolled over on her left side and closed her eyes, waiting for sleep to come over her.

* * *

Chapter 7

Elena's face dropped as she read the four names on the list.

Sara Evens

Thomas Golby

George Tewell

Hannah Overton

Those were the coordinators chosen for the DEA operation. Elena's name was missing from the list. She couldn't believe it. She'd thought her application had been great, but she guessed it wasn't good enough for this program. She turned to Paige and Patrick.

"I didn't get it," she said simply.

Paige looked forlorn. "I'm sorry, Elena. I know how much you wanted this."

"I just wanted to be a part of something that would really make a difference to people. I wanted to be a doer instead of just a learner."

She shrugged. "I guess it wasn't meant to be. At least I can still be part of the project as an investigator with you."

"Yea," Paige said.

"And if you don't want to do it, you don't have to," Patrick advised. "Maybe take this first semester to get accustomed to the program and get into the swing of things?"

"No," Elena said firmly. "If I can't be one of the coordinators, I can at least investigate for the DEA. It's not the same, but it's better than nothing."

"Alright," Paige said, "let's get going. We're going to be late for the meeting."

"Might as well meet the coordinators that we'll be working with for the project," Elena said.

Patrick started walking down the hallway towards the small conference room. The list of coordinator names was pinned on the wall in the hall that was part of the Professional Student Conference area. No one else was lingering by the sign except Paige, Elena, and Patrick. The rest of the Professional Students were already in their next session – either a breakout session, or getting ready for the orientation to the DEA project to start in the small conference room where Paige, Elena, and Patrick were headed now.

They took their seats at the back of the room. There were about thirty Professional Students sitting in the audience. Mark, Hal, and Frank were standing at the front of the room, along with two men and one woman, who Elena guessed were three of the coordinators.

Hal stepped forward to the podium. Frank and Mark stood in the background. Hal's gray hair was glowing in the light above them. Mark's glasses were reflecting light as well. Frank looked dark in comparison, with his brown hair, tan skin, and all black suit.

"Hello, everyone," Hal called out. "Let's get started."

He walked across the front of the room, behind the podium, back and forth, pacing slowly. "You all know why you're here," he said. "You've chosen to be a part of a very important operation, and we couldn't be more pleased with the turnout of volunteers." He smiled.

"I'll turn this over to my colleagues, Mark and Frank to explain the protocol for the operation. But first, I'd like to introduce the coordinators for the project." He gestured towards the two tall men and the long and lanky woman sitting toward the front of the room. All three of them looked serious. The man on the left wore a blue button-down shirt with khaki pants. The other was wearing a navy suit with a white shirt underneath the jacket. The woman, who looked like she had been stretched out like Gumby, was sitting with her legs crossed in a professional black dress – quite formal.

"This is Thomas, George, and Hannah – three of the coordinators for the operation."

The three coordinators waved at the audience, acknowledging their introduction, though they didn't appear to be getting up or saying anything to the crowd.

Elena, Paige, and Patrick clapped politely along with the rest of the Professional Students in the audience. Elena listened as Mark and Frank explained the protocol for the operation. Frank was very forthcoming, explaining everything carefully, clearly for everyone to understand. Mark was hurried. He glossed over some of the specifics that Frank then clarified in the next breath.

They talked about how there would be check-ins between the investigators and the coordinators every two days. How the weekend conferences would be reserved for this project's meetings for them from now on. That all of this was still completely optional and they could choose not to participate if they changed their minds.

Then Hal stepped forward again. He was looking at his watch on his right wrist. "We actually had a fourth coordinator selected, but it seems that she is not coming to the meeting today, which means she is out of the position," he said sternly. "We may select a fourth coordinator today if we feel that there is a good fit," Hal explained.

Elena only had one thing on her mind – *there was one coordinator position left. She still had a chance.* She perked up at the thought of this and listened carefully to Hal as he wrapped up the meeting.

"Please look at the groups listed on the board in the back of the room, which tell you which room to go to next. We have broken you up into four groups of ten or nine individuals. This will be your 'unit'. Each unit will report together each week at the upcoming conferences to work together on this project. You will share experiences with your unit and you will share a coordinator. That being said, we will determine if we need to combine the fourth unit by the end of today if we don't select another coordinator."

The Professional Students stood up and made their way to the back of the room. Elena, Paige, and Patrick were at the back of the pack.

Elena found her name in group four, under the fourth coordinator's name, who was no longer with them. She wondered who would lead her group today. Paige and Patrick were in group one, George's group.

George led his group to the front left side of the room, Thomas led his group to the front right, and Hannah led her flock to the back left. The final group of Professional Students was left standing in the middle of the room, waiting for instructions, when Mark stepped over to the back right corner and raised his hand.

"Over here, group four!" he called. "I'm filling in as coordinator today. And, if we select a new coordinator, it will

74

be from your group. That was part of the reason we put you all in group four – you all applied to be coordinators – and we wanted all of the applicants together in case something like this happened."

There were ten of them in the group. They sat in a circle of chairs, with Mark in the middle. He pushed up his glasses over his nose and cracked his knuckles in preparation.

"Let's get started," he said to all of them. "We're going to do an ice breaker activity."

Mark passed around a bowl with pieces of folded up paper inside and each Professional Student took one piece of paper. They didn't unfold the paper until Mark told them to, so they didn't know what was on it.

"Ok," Mark said, when everyone had picked a piece, "I'm going to take a volunteer and you're going to open your paper, and pick a person to ask the question to. Everyone will get a chance to answer a question," he explained.

"Margaret," Mark said, pointing to the average-looking woman sitting to Elena's left. "You start."

She stood up without being asked and opened her paper.

"Ok," she said. "I'm going to ask...you," she said pointing at the man directly across from her.

"Which university are you taking classes at this semester?" Margaret asked. "And which class is your favorite?"

"First introduce yourself for any of the new Professional Students in this group – I think we only have one actually," Mark said. He gestured at Elena. "This is Elena," he said, and everybody smiled and waved.

"Nice to meet you," several people said to Elena in unison.

"Nice to meet all of you too," she replied happily.

"Ok," Mark said. "Now that that's out of the way, Adam?"

The man stood up. "Hi," he said, "I'm Adam Worth," he said looking right at Elena, since she was the only person who didn't know him.

"I'm taking classes at Yale this semester, and my favorite class so far is Philosophy of Harry Potter," he said without hesitation. "I'm a huge Harry Potter nerd," he said. He pulled up the bottom of his left pant leg to reveal a Gryffindor sock. "In case you couldn't tell." He smirked.

"Great," Mark said. "Now, Adam, you pick the next person."

Adam's brow furrowed as he seemed to be making a difficult decision. Then he looked at Elena and their eyes locked. "Elena, you're next," he said. He unfolded his paper and flattened it out on his hand.

"Why did you choose to get involved with this special project?" he asked.

Elena pondered the question, but only for a few seconds before she responded. "I've always been in the background." She paused. "In school, I was at the top of my class, but never the best. I was the good girl who always played by the rules. That's how I was with my family too. My family relies on me to do the right thing and support myself – to keep things stable. But with this, this is different. I have the chance to really do something worthwhile and to actually do something rather than just think. I want to make a difference in the world like I never have before. And I want to help people who can't help themselves," she said simply.

There was silence around the circle.

"Did I say something stupid?" Elena asked innocently.

"No," Adam said. "There was absolutely nothing stupid about that response," he said. "I think you just took us all by surprise. We weren't expecting you to be so invested in your first project."

"Well," Elena said, "there's more to the story." She bit her lip as she thought how to explain.

"My cousin ended up hanging out with a bad crowd in college. They convinced him to start using heroin and he overdosed when he was 21."

Everyone just stared at her in amazement, and pity.

"He was one of my best friends," Elena said.

"No one in my family talks about it, but it's made me really determined to prevent drug use in young adults." One tear fell on Elena's cheek – she wiped it off swiftly.

Mark took a couple of steps toward Elena and put his hand on her right shoulder and squeezed. "I get it," he said honestly.

Then Mark stepped back. "Elena, you're the new coordinator," he said suddenly.

The group in the circle started to applaud, and slowly but surely the applause spread throughout the rest of the room – everyone had been listening to their group.

Elena looked around, flustered, and then met Paige's eyes. Paige just clapped, made eye contact, and nodded as if she was agreeing to an important condition.

Elena's eyes swept the room and she caught a glimpse of Patrick too – he looked solemn. His eyes were stoic and his mouth was straight. His left hand was clasping Paige's right, as if he would never let go.

Frank and Mark had made their way to the center of the room while Elena was looking around.

"Well," Frank said with a smile, "we have our last coordinator."

"I think we'll have the investigators continue with this exercise and I want to talk to the four coordinators in my office,"

Frank said confidently.

Thomas, George, Hannah, and Elena walked up to Frank and Mark and followed Frank out of the hall. Mark remained in the room with the others.

"Ok!" he called. "Everyone back to their groups!"

Elena looked back at Paige and Patrick before she stepped out the door. The four coordinators and the DEA leader were making their way down the hotel hallway towards the back office, quietly.

They entered the office at the end of the hallway on the left, where they found a long table with four seats. Frank clicked his tongue as he stepped to the front of the room and gathered his thoughts. The four coordinators took their seats at the table and silence fell in the room.

Frank walked over to his desk and pulled out a packet of papers. He proceeded to hand them out to the four coordinators seated at the table. Elena took her packet and looked at the front page –

DEA Coordinator Policies

Please read the following rules and regulations and either agree to the policies or dismiss yourself from this responsibility promptly...

It went on for a couple of pages with numbered rules for how they should behave as a coordinator for the DEA. Mostly, the rules encompassed issues of confidentiality. They would agree to speak to no one outside of the Professional Student Program about the DEA project and only speak with their supervisor about any findings from their individual sessions with the investigators.

Elena, Thomas, George, and Hannah skimmed the pages of

the document, reading each word quickly, simply wanting to agree to the statements set forth and begin their journey with the DEA.

Elena finished reading and looked up at the others. George was tapping his fingers on the table, Hannah was crossing and uncrossing her legs. Everyone was getting antsy. Frank had sat down at his desk and started reading over some papers that were sitting out. Elena wondered what he was studying so closely. He looked like he was completely immersed in what he was reading, while the four coordinators were nearly jumping out of their seats with excitement.

Finally, after what seemed like hours to Elena and the others, Frank stood up from his desk and asked them to sign the document if they agreed. In that instant, all four coordinators picked up the pen that was sitting at their side and signed the document, without any hesitation.

Frank raised his eyebrows as he watched all four individuals get up promptly and hand him their papers. Not one person had stopped to consider whether this was a bad idea. It seemed they were all sold on the DEA project.

Frank wasn't surprised about Hannah, George, and Thomas – they were senior Professional Students – they had been in the program for years now – but he was still a little unsure of Elena. She was the only new PS to be selected as a coordinator, and she wasn't even selected at first, he thought. Mark was intrigued by her, Frank decided. He would need to go along with Mark's decision, but Frank doubted that Elena could handle this responsibility. She was too mousy to succeed as a coordinator – she would be better suited for a background job, one where she could just follow instructions like a good girl.

But Frank kept these thoughts to himself. He ran his hand

through his long brown hair, tousling it in the process, thinking hard about how he could make sure this project succeeded.

"Well," he said, "that's it. Let's get started." And he turned to the whiteboard behind him and started to write and draw. He was showing them the plan of action. Who would be in their respective groups, the format of their individual sessions, and everything Frank knew about the current standing of the college drug ring. He had to give them a crash course in DEA policies, of course, but what he was most concerned with was their critical thinking abilities.

He would need to feel out the group to see who would be best suited for this role. He sensed George would be a good fit. He was large, muscular, loud, obtrusive – he made an entrance – no one would think of messing with him. That's who Frank had his money on. But he droned on with his speech and watched as the four young coordinators took notes and raised their hands to ask questions throughout the session.

By the end of the session, Frank was fairly certain that they were all up to par. They knew what they needed to do and if they hadn't gotten up and left when they heard about the violence that may ensue when approaching the accused, he decided that he would have to put his faith in this group. He would have to help them as much as he could to ensure they succeeded with the mission. Though he felt a twinge of envy. These PS's would have the fun job. They would get to go out and do things, while he, Frank, would be stuck pushing papers behind a desk. At least he'd have Mark to help him through this. And, maybe if he played his cards right, he would have another project like this in the future with Mark by his side, though Mark had been acting strange lately, as if he was going somewhere. Maybe he was taking a trip. But maybe he was being reassigned to another project. That could be it. It he was reassigned, it would be top secret until the announcement about the new project came out. Well, Frank would have to be on the lookout for changes upcoming. He couldn't deal with losing Mark, not now, but if Mark had a better opportunity who was he to stop him?

As Frank argued in his head with himself, he realized the four coordinators had fallen silent.

"Is that all?" George asked expectantly.

Frank hadn't realized he finished talking and wiped down the board already. He was walking toward the door and the others were still in their seats.

"Yes," he said, shaking his head of his thoughts. "You're free to go."

They were on the edge of their seats, waiting for their dismissal and they promptly rose from their chairs and filed out of the room.

"Thank you," Elena said to Frank as she stepped out the door.

"Yes, thanks," Hannah echoed.

Frank thought, this was going to be a worthwhile project. He was excited to be working with this group. Now, for the start of the mission, the coordinating, the investigating, the sleuthing.

Chapter 8

"Paige," Elena said on the phone to her friend, "I still can't believe you were assigned to my investigator group. This feels strange."

"I know," Paige replied. "I feel like we're just talking about everyday stuff, but it's really all about something so serious. So...coordinator...what do we need to talk about this week?"

"You know I don't have a set agenda," Elena said. "This is all about what came up for you."

"Of course, well it's a whole lot of nothing," Paige said. "It's just a normal college class with normal students and a normal professor – nothing out of the ordinary," she stated.

"Ok, well tell me about some of the students," Elena probed. "Do any of them stand out to you?"

"There's this one guy, Bill, he smokes in the parking lot, but it's just a cigarette – nothing serious. I think he's harmless.

"And they're always talking about trading Shadow cards," she continues. "But that's the whole Bill crew. They're all in the D&D club and the Harry Potter Fan group. They love all that sci-fi and fantasy stuff."

"Hey!" Elena said. "Don't dis Harry Potter!"

Paige giggled. She knew she could get Elena up in arms about HP any day of the week.

Paige sat in her bedroom, talking on the phone to Elena, with the Zoom video playing in the background. They all had to dial in by phone on the PS conference line for their coordinator sessions. It was annoying, but Paige knew it was all about privacy and confidentiality – she understood their zeal for discretion.

She tapped her fingers on her desk, one at a time, thinking about what she would say to Elena next. She knew her friend wanted to solve this case. She knew Elena wanted to make a difference with the DEA, but so far there had been no leads from any of the coordinators. Paige doubted they would find out anything soon, but she wanted to support her friend, so she continued to talk about the group of students in her class who played with the Shadow cards and talked about Harry Potter nonstop.

"I learned that I'm a Ravenclaw," she said at last. "Bill told me I'm cunning and witty. That I can figure out any puzzle," Paige explained.

"Well, it's true," Elena told her. "You're very smart – you have a way of getting to the bottom of every problem. I wouldn't doubt it if you figured out who was behind this DEA crime on your own, to be honest."

"No way," Paige said honestly. "You're the leader here. I'm just following orders. I've never been one to take charge of a project. I always fall into the background. I'll tell you what I know, but I won't take it a step further and act," she said truthfully.

"Then why did you sign up?" Elena asked.

"Because I wanted to be there for you," she said simply.

"Well," Elena paused, "thanks. I appreciate the support for my first project.

"And thanks for showing me the ropes with all the PS special projects," she said. "I couldn't have done this without you – and Patrick."

"You're welcome!" Elena heard Patrick call from the background. He and Paige were living together in their cozy one-bedroom apartment in Southern California, near San Diego. They commuted to the University of Southern California for their classes. But it was the winter break right now, a week before Christmas and the students were all left to their own devices while the professors took a hard-earned break from teaching. But the PS's didn't get a break. They were instructed to wander about the campus, keeping their eyes open and ears attuned for anything unusual that might occur in the absence of faculty. And, they also had their weekly leadership workshops. Their next one was that coming weekend – Elena couldn't wait to see Paige and Patrick in person again! It had been a couple of weeks; they had to cancel the last workshop because Mark was out sick.

"Have you heard about the next project yet?" Paige asked. "I think they were going to announce something at our next workshop."

"Oh yeah, Mark told me he was announcing it soon but he wouldn't tell us anything else about it yet. Said the policy is for all the PS's to find out together," Elena said offhandedly.

Then she wondered, did Paige know something that she didn't? Was Mark giving some of the PS's extra information. It seemed like Paige had brought up the subject of the special projects for a reason. Was she trying to hint to Elena that she knew more than her?

Stop it, Elena chastised herself. Paige was her friend. She wouldn't hide things from her. *I'm just being paranoid. It's been happening a lot lately,* she thought. For a while she was thinking that something was up with Mark and Frank. She kept catching them talking in their offices before her supervisor meetings, and she caught Mark on the phone sounding really put off the other day.

He said it was family stuff though. She guessed it made sense – this whole experience was so damn surreal. She hadn't really questioned the reality of everything until now. Was this all a hoax? Was she actually working for the DEA?

Of course she was, she told herself calmly. She had seen all the official paperwork from the PS program and the DEA. She had been getting her biweekly paychecks directly deposited into her bank account. She had state health insurance – all of that pretty much confirmed that this was a real job. But why did she still harbor an inkling somewhere way in the back of her mind that something was wrong?

Well, she thought, there was a lot wrong. They hadn't made any progress with the DEA project yet. However, there was a student at Paige's school who overdosed recently. The campus tried to keep the whole incident hushed up, but Paige did learn some information about that. They had talked about it at their last coordinator session. Maybe Elena should bring it up again? It can't hurt, she thought, as Paige went on in the background talking to Patrick about dinner.

"Hey, Paige?" She cut off her friend midsentence.

"Yeah?" she asked uncertainly.

"Whatever happened with that overdose you heard about last week and the University? Any news?"

"Oh yeah, I almost forgot," Paige said quickly. Elena sensed a nervous energy to her friend in that moment. "It never even appeared in the newspaper or anything. But I heard a little more from Sarah's friend in my Philosophy class."

"Go on," Elena prompted her.

"Sarah's friend, Ashley – the girl I started being friends with – she said that Sarah is still in the hospital recovering. But she really didn't want to tell me anything else. Said Sarah got mixed up in the wrong crowd and she didn't really know how it happened. She started acting a little differently after she got back from her trip to see her twin sister at Yale the other week. Ashley asked her if something happened, and Sarah just said they had an argument."

"Well," Elena said, "this is the only lead we have so far. And that's using the word 'lead' loosely. We don't actually know anything about the situation except Sarah's condition and the bit of background about her recent activities. But I guess that's more than we've had before."

"Yeah," Paige mumbled, "that's all I know – sorry."

"Don't apologize," Elena said. "This is helpful." She took more notes and stopped her recording that she had started when Paige explained the situation. Elena would be reporting back to Mark and Frank tomorrow, Friday night before the leadership workshop. The coordinators all travelled back to New York the day prior to the workshop for their one-on-one meetings with the supervisors before all the other PS's arrived.

After Elena hung up the phone with Paige, she started to organize her things. There were papers all over her apartment, scattered on the floor, on the coffee table, the couch, the kitchen counters...

She had so many notes and policies from the DEA that she really needed to file, but Elena had always been a bit scattered when it came to documents. She vowed to get a filing cabinet this weekend on her way back from the conference. She moved about the apartment, trying to grab any papers in sight - scraps, full notepads, packets – she piled them all up on the dining room table and stuck a large vase on top of the pile to hold it in place.

She looked around. No more papers on the floor – that was a start, she thought. She had definitely been neglecting her housekeeping and organizing for the past week. The coordinator position took up more of her energy than she originally thought it would. She had just finished up her Psychology classes at Yale – Elena's Christmas break started Tuesday. She took her last final exam on Monday afternoon. Dr. Likert wished her a happy new year and she and Elena exchanged small gifts after the exam. They had gotten especially close this past month. Dr. Likert was like an older sister that Elena never had. Although she knew about the professional student program, she didn't know about the DEA project, so she just thought Elena was training for a leadership position.

She was grooming Elena for a Psychologist career. She thought Elena had what it took to be a clinical psychologist at a hospital, which is what Dr. Likert had done herself before she started teaching at Yale. She still worked at the local hospital per diem now, filling in for the head Psychologist once a month for his regularly scheduled vacations.

Elena snapped herself back to the present, as she tried to flatten the pile of papers on her dining room table. She didn't need to show anyone these papers – they were just her notes and for her records – but she decided that she wanted to start to be more organized in the new year, especially now that she was a coordinator for her first project.

* * *

Elena was getting her bags ready for her drive and loading the car when her phone rang.

"Hello?" she answered.

"Elena, it's Hal."

"Oh, hi," she started, unsure of why he was calling her – she was just getting ready to go meet with Mark and Frank – why would Hal be calling her?

"It's about Mark," he said. "He's fallen ill again. He apologizes but he needs to cancel your meeting tonight and he's calling off this week's conference too."

"Is everything ok?" she asked uncertainly. Mark had been sick the other week – the flu, they said – she wondered what was wrong now.

"Oh yes," Hal said, shiftily, "just a cold or something. Nothing to worry about. But do tell your PS investigators not to come to the conference. I've been charged with calling the coordinators to alert them of the change of events."

"Alright," Elena said solemnly, "so no check-in this week? Are we at least doing a phone call, me, Mark and Frank?"

"Afraid not," Hal said. "But you can tell me anything you found out from your investigators this week and I'll pass along the message to the team."

"Well..." she said. "I did take down some notes from my meeting with Paige yesterday that I wanted to review, but maybe it would be better for you to just have Mark and Frank call me when they feel up to it?"

"No, no," Hal assured her. "Time is of the essence with this case. We haven't been making much progress and every piece of information helps."

She closed her car door, resigned that she was no longer leaving her apartment. "Let me call you back in a few minutes," she said. "I was just loading up the car to drive down there when you called. I just want to put some of my stuff back inside and get to my room before I discuss some of this," she said in a hushed tone.

"Fine," he said. Elena thought she heard a hint of annoyance in his voice. She was about to ask him what was wrong, or apologize for any inconvenience, when Hal said quickly, "Bye. Call me back at this number when you're ready. And don't forget to tell your investigators about the cancellation too."

He hung up suddenly. Elena was left wondering what was wrong with Hal. He'd always seemed like he liked Elena. Lately, she hadn't been seeing him at the conferences though. He didn't seem to be as involved in the DEA project as Mark and Frank.

"Different assignments," Mark had explained one day when Elena inquired about Hal's lack of presence at the workshops.

"His boss is starting to pull him onto different projects in other departments now. He seems rather put off about it, to tell you the truth."

But that was all Mark had told Elena, and assuming it was a touchy subject for her supervisors, she decided to stay away from that topic of conversation in the future.

But now that she hung up with Hal, she wondered why he was suddenly making the phone calls for Mark and Frank. Maybe he was back on the project?

Seems kind of strange, Elena thought. But then she shook her head, trying to clear it – enough, she thought. Why am I so paranoid?

She had been on edge the past few days. Actually, since the overdose at Paige's school, to be honest. Things had been different for her since then. She thought maybe it reminded her of her cousin. As she thought of this, she had to hold back a sigh. She thought she was over this by now, but the overdose this past week resurfaced all the feelings she had from last year with her cousin. Her family never talked about it, but Elena knew that everyone was broken up about what happened. Things weren't the same after that. Maybe that's why Elena's mom didn't talk to her sisters anymore. It was easier to ignore the problem than to face it, she guessed.

But Elena wasn't going to turn into her mother. She wasn't going to let this eat away at her for the rest of her life. Instead, she was going to face the problem head on.

Elena looked in the top drawer of the desk in her room. She rummaged through old receipts, her checkbook, a journal, until she found the business card she was looking for.

Dr. Julia Steinhert

Psychotherapist, Psychologist, LCSW

Elena hesitated as she read the name on the card. Mark had given this to her, as well as to the other coordinators, at their last meeting.

"Times are getting tough," he said. "There's a lot of pressure on everyone, and we want you all to know that there are resources you can reach out to."

He handed them each a stack of business cards.

"These are for the Psychologist on staff at the Department of Learning. She's really great. All of the supervisors had to go through extensive therapy with her before being promoted to our current positions – screening process. She can be a great asset to you as a Professional Student," he assured Elena, specifically.

Elena had thrown the card in the bottom of her book bag and when she got home, she buried it in her desk drawer, assuming

90

she would never take it out. Though she was sure to hand out the other cards to her investigators during their one-on-ones. She assured them all that this was confidential and they could call Dr. Steinhert if they wished, free of charge, through the DOL.

While the investigators seemed grateful overall, Paige was the one who seemed actually relieved by the card, Elena remembered.

Then, Elena thought, Paige had never told her during their conversation yesterday if she'd called Dr. Steinhart. She hadn't mentioned the psychotherapist at all since the day Elena gave her the card, but Elena didn't want to push her friend to disclose anything she wasn't ready to talk about.

Now, as Elena held the business card in both hands, staring at the phone number for Dr. Steinhart, she wondered if this was exactly what her friend had done last week when Elena gave her a card. Did Paige go through the same motions and then decide to call Dr. Steinhart? Or, did she decide against reaching out for professional help?

Elena didn't want to guess what her good friend would do, but instead she thought about what was right for herself. She was on edge lately. She probably should acknowledge that, as it could start interfering with her career if she wasn't careful. Elena loved her job as a coordinator for the Professional Students program and she didn't want anything to jeopardize her standing there.

Therefore, she swallowed her pride and made the phone call. Despite being a psychology major, Elena still believed some of the common stereotypes about going to therapy – that it could make you weak, that you're admitting you have a problem – but she fought the urge to beat herself up and instead tried to tell herself that she was brave for reaching out.

The phone rang, and rang, and then it went to Dr. Steinhart's voicemail.

"Hello, this is Julia Steinhert. I can't get to the phone right now because I'm either with a client or out of the office, but please leave a message and I'll be sure to get back to you as soon as I can."

Beep.

"Um..." Elena hesitated. "Hi." She paused. "I'm Elena Brooks and I'm part of the Professional Student program through the DOL. Mark Sampson gave me your card because he thought maybe I should set up a session with you." She thought for a minute about how to proceed.

"You see," she said, "I'm a coordinator for my first special project, and I think it's really starting to take a toll on me. So, I guess...I just need someone to talk to. So, if you could give me a call back when you get a chance, I'd like to set up a session. Um...thanks. Bye," she ended awkwardly.

Well, now with that out of the way, Elena figured she better call Hal back. But, she thought, maybe she should wait until after Dr. Steinhert called her to set up a session. Or until after she had a session with her and talked about how she was feeling. But she couldn't wait, she decided. Hal had said this was urgent. They needed all the information they could get about the DEA project and Elena didn't want to hold back anything that could help them gain traction.

She whipped out her phone again, sat down in the chair at her desk and leaned back, propping up her feet on the bottom wooden beam of the desk. She was as relaxed as she was going to get, she thought.

She dialed Hal's number and waited for him to answer. The

phone barely rang once before he promptly responded, "Hello? Elena?"

She was taken aback by how concerned he sounded. "Is everything ok?" she asked.

He cleared his throat. "Yes, of course," he said. "Why wouldn't it be?"

"Well, you just sound a little...never mind," Elena said. "Is now a good time to talk?"

"Yes, yes," he muttered. "Now is great."

"What about Frank?" Elena asked. "Don't you want to conference him in?"

"Oh no, Frank is busy right now," Hal mumbled. "Serious business for the DEA, top secret," he said as if that explained everything.

"Um...ok," Elena said. "Well, it's not much, but I just wanted to let you know that I had my one-on-one with Paige and she gave me a little more information about the overdose that happened last week at her school. It seems like she got to know a friend of the girl."

"Go on," Hal prompted her, clearly interested. Maybe he was taking notes for Frank and Mark, she thought.

"Well, she said something about the girl Sarah getting caught up with a 'bad crowd' after she came back from visiting her sister at Yale. Said she and the sister got into some sort of argument and she wasn't the same after that. The next week she overdosed. The friend said she had no idea Sarah ever did drugs either. The whole thing seems a little off, don't you think?" Elena wondered aloud.

The line was silent on Hal's end for a moment. Then he said, "So that's all Paige told you? Nothing else?" he pried.

Elena had the sense that Hal was waiting for more, but she

didn't know what else to tell him. Maybe she was just being paranoid again. Maybe Hal was just trying to be thorough, she thought. Or maybe, maybe he knew something more. But Elena tried to let that thought go as she assured Hal, "No, that's all."

He let out a disappointed sigh. Elena felt a twinge of guilt for not being able to help more, though she thought that her information would be helpful and she'd hoped that when she told Mark and Frank they would be happy for information about the incident at Paige's school. She was fooling herself, though. Hal wanted more information. He wouldn't be content with a nugget of knowledge that didn't bring them any closer to the leader of the drug ring. Elena felt deflated. She couldn't believe she had been stupid enough to think that she would receive praise for this information. She hadn't even put any pieces of the puzzle together, and it was sort of like a puzzle, she thought. She would just have to try harder. She would do more investigating by talking with Paige and the other PS investigators. She would take notes diligently. She would even visit the other school campuses is she had to – she would do whatever might be necessary to make more progress on this project, she decided.

When she hung up with Hal, she had the feeling that he was disappointed in her, but she didn't let that get her down. She would just do better going forward. Maybe a call from Dr. Steinhert would be welcoming after this weekend's turn of events – no workshop, no meeting with Mark and Frank, little information to report, disappointment from Hal – yes, she thought. She would welcome a call from a professional with an outsider's perspective on the situation, someone who knew about the Professional Student special projects and she could confide in without worrying about breaching confidentiality.

Yes, she would just have to wait until Dr. Steinhert returned her call, and then she could decide how she would proceed. Until then, Elena would get some rest. It was getting late and she finished bringing her bags back into her apartment and unpacking her things. Now she would get ready for bed, though it was only 8:00 p.m. Maybe she would read some Harry Potter in bed before she dozed off. That would take her mind of things, she thought.

She pulled on her loungewear, which she used as her pajamas for the night, brushed her teeth, washed her face, and used the bathroom in a rush before she tucked herself into her bed comfortably with her book. It was dark in the bedroom, because she had turned off the light when she came in. But she quickly flicked on the lamp switch on her nightstand and a halo of light shone over her, allowing her to read her favorite book for a little while as she eased her way into a hopefully dreamless, restful sleep.

Chapter 9

The sun rose Saturday morning in Elena's window like a blaring siren that she couldn't turn off. It was 7:00 and although she laid down last night around 8:00, she had ended up reading Harry Potter late into the night. It was 1:00 a.m. before she put the book down, turned off the lamp and shut her eyes. It seemed a bit too early to be awake, but Elena was never one to sleep in on the weekend. Of course, when she was at the PS conferences over the weekends, she had to wake up extra early to get started by 7:00 in the morning, so this was already kind of late by comparison.

She sat up, stretched her arms over her head and let out a long yawn. She blinked a few times to clear her eyes and then she grabbed her glasses from the nightstand, clearing up the room in her field of vision. She shielded her eyes from the light peeking in through her window now, determined to slowly wake up and enjoy a relaxing day off. She decided to get up out of bed and head to the kitchen to make some coffee and breakfast.

She slowly slumped her way to the kitchen and immediately pressed the button to run the coffeemaker. She had set it up last night, as usual. Thankful that she wouldn't have to wait long, Elena slowly opened the refrigerator door, hesitantly, unsure of what she would find inside – she hadn't gone food shopping yesterday. She was pleasantly surprised to find a four pack of Greek yogurts and when she checked the freezer she saw that she had a bag of frozen blueberries. She then quickly searched the cabinet and found a box of oatmeal. Perfect, she thought – just enough to get me through breakfast. Then she peered back in the fridge and noticed the container of cold cuts in the drawer and a spare tortilla – maybe she could even put off food shopping until after lunch today.

Beep. Beep – beep.

Elena quickly assembled her breakfast and then turned to the coffeemaker, the source of the noise and sighed in relief as she noticed the pot was full of fresh coffee. She smiled, picked up her bowl of oatmeal, mixed with yogurt and blueberries, placed it on the table and then rushed back to the counter to grab her first cup of coffee of the day.

She sat back in her wooden chair, feet resting on the wooden beam under the seat in front of her, and took a sip of much-needed coffee.

"Ahh," she said happily after she swallowed the black coffee.

She took out her phone and started reading some articles on Reddit, her typical relaxing morning routine.

There wasn't much she was interested in today. Sure, there was the typical political hype surrounding the new presidency, but that was becoming old news, to be honest. There was a new iPhone that just got released for Christmas. Elena spent a few minutes reading up on the new specs, and after seeing the price tag, decided that her current phone worked just fine.

It was 9:00 by the time she finished her two cups of coffee, her breakfast, and her reading. She jumped up, scurried to the bedroom and grabbed her clothes, then headed to the bathroom to take a nice warm shower.

The warm water hit her skin, like a candle being held right above the skin. It was great, especially since this week it just started getting really cold out. It dropped into the 20s last night! Elena didn't dilly dally in the shower, but instead quickly warmed up, and then got out and got dressed for the day. She ran a brush through her smooth, chocolate brown hair, dripping wet from just getting out of the shower.

She used her towel to try to dry off her hair a bit more before she picked up the hairdryer. She hesitated, thinking she might not leave the apartment today; she decided against spending time drying her hair and instead braided it to the side of her head – it would dry eventually, she reasoned.

Elena didn't feel like putting any makeup on today – it was a lounging day. She was wearing her Ravenclaw sweatpants with a blue sweater. Her socks were striped with blue and purple, soft and warm, and her slippers were gray with fur along the edges.

She glanced at her reflection in the mirror and thought she looked a little pale. She knew she was getting stressed out the past couple of weeks and it was finally starting to show with her dry skin and the dark bags under her eyes. Though she got 1:30 a.m.-7a.m., she felt like her sleep was interrupted last night. She had some strange dreams that kept her tossing and turning, though she couldn't remember the details anymore. Something related to the DEA project, as usual. She didn't have to be a dream expert to know that this was because her job was always on her mind these days, and she knew it wasn't great all the time, but she loved it so much, it seemed like the stress would be worth it in the end, especially after finally solving this first case for the DEA.

But Adam, her cousin, was on her mind today. She wondered

if he had gotten mixed up in something like this in college. Was he pressured to do drugs? Was he tricked into it by older students who were trying to manipulate him? Could Elena have made a difference if she knew what was going on at the time?

She had so many questions, and it seemed like she never got any answers. Of course, her family wouldn't answer any of her questions about Adam – they just pretended nothing happened and they avoided the topic of drugs at all cost. Elena knew she couldn't talk to her mom about what she was going through, because her mom didn't even know about the DEA project. How could Elena explain why she was suddenly thinking about Adam all the time, when her mom had no idea that her job was involved with getting to the bottom of a drug ring for the DEA? She knew she couldn't disclose any of the confidential information. And, it was killing her that she couldn't tell Jodi either, but in this moment, she really wished she could actually talk to her mom. Despite pretending that everything with Adam didn't happen, Elena knew her mom would have understood Elena's mixed emotions about the DEA project if she explained, because her mom had a personal connection to the issue too, no matter how hard she tried to ignore it and push it away.

This, Elena thought, was why Mark had suggested that she talk to Dr. Steinhert. Elena felt a mixture of relief and unease, hoping that Dr. Steinhert would give her a call soon, but wondering whether it would really help her. She had to hope. That was all she could do at this point.

And then, Elena heard her phone ringing. She was still in the bathroom, stuck in her thoughts, but she was ripped from the reverie by the ringing. She ran into the kitchen, hoping that this was Dr. Steinhert returning her call, when she saw the unknown number on her phone. Could this be her? she wondered.

She didn't hesitate. She picked up the phone eagerly. "Hello, this is Elena," she answered promptly.

"Hello, Elena. I'm Julia, Julia Steinhert – you called me yesterday about setting up an appointment and I was just returning your call. Do you have a few minutes to talk?"

"Yes, of course," Elena said. "I don't really know how this works," she started. "I mean, I studied Psychology in college and I took a bunch of counseling classes, so I actually know a lot about therapy," she rambled, "but I don't know the protocol for working with a Psychologist through the DOL. I've never had to seek therapy for myself, so this is really new for me to be on the receiving end of the treatment."

Dr. Steinhert laughed lightheartedly. "Understandable," she said. "How about I just gather some of the preliminary information so we can get you set up as a new client?"

"That sounds good," Elena said with a sigh of relief.

"Ok, so your name is Elena Brooks? Date of birth?"

"Yes, and 1/31/97."

"So you're 23, turning 24?"

"Yes, that's right," Elena said.

"Address?" She paused. "Or does your job at the DOL require you to move around a lot?"

"I mean," Elena started, "I think I'll have to move around a lot but I haven't moved yet. Do you just want my current address?"

"Yes, please, and past addresses for the past five years."

"That will be 5 Burlow Lane Apt C New Haven, CT 06501. And for my past address, I live with my parents at 44 Halots Rd. Smithtown, NY 11787."

Dr. Steinhert paused and Elena could hear her typing in the background, she assumed she was taking notes or filling out the paperwork.

"Now, what is your role at the DOL?" Dr. Steinhert asked.

"I'm a Professional Student coordinator for the DEA project 05481 – College drug ring. I work under Mark Sampson and Frank Furlow," she said calmly. "Oh yeah – and Hal Trinup," she added.

"Oh, of course," Dr. Steinhert said. "Mark is great! He's always referring people to me, and rightfully so with your line of work," she said seriously.

"So what brings you to therapy?" Dr. Steinhert asked openly.

"Well, now that I'm a coordinator for the DEA project, I'm starting to exhibit some signs of excessive stress," she confessed. "I noticed that I'm not really sleeping much and I'm having bad dreams most nights. I think it's because I kind of have a personal connection to drug problems in college. A cousin of mine died from an overdose a few years ago, and I never really dealt with it, but this project is bringing up a lot of...uncomfortable feelings, I guess," she said in a rush.

"I see," Dr. Steinhert said, typing noises rushing through the background of the phone call. "Well, this all sounds like a straightforward case," Dr. Steinhert said. "You say you've never sought therapy in the past?"

"No. Never," Elena said.

"Ok, well this is going to be an adjustment for you probably. I would think as a PS you're an overachiever, used to getting everything right the first time you try – am I correct?" she asked expectantly.

"Yes, that's accurate," Elena admitted sheepishly.

"I'm going to lay out a plan for your treatment," Dr. Steinhert said. "I suggest meeting once every week for one 45-minute session. If we need to increase or decrease the frequency of the sessions we certainly can, but I think this is a good starting point. And I'm not sure if Mark told you, but this is covered 100% by your health insurance with the DOL – it's part of our employee assistance program. You get 25 sessions a year and anything past that is subject to a $15 copay, which I can assure you, is very good considering the health insurance plans with other employers nowadays," she finished.

"That's all fine with me," Elena said. "When do we start?" she asked innocently.

"I have openings this Thursday, next Saturday, and next Sunday. Do any of those days work for you?"

"The weekends would probably be best – actually, no, because that's when we usually have our conferences." She paused. "How about Thursday? What times do you have open?"

"Do you want the morning or the evening?"

"It's my school's break," Elena said, "so I don't have classes to work around, but I guess for going forward the evening would be better because I typically have classes in the morning."

"Does 5:30 p.m. work for you?" Dr. Steinhert asked promptly.

"Yes, that's perfect," Elena responded hopefully, feeling like there might finally be a light at the end of this dark tunnel of the past two weeks.

"I'll send you a text reminder the day before our appointment," Dr. Steinhert said. "Is this the best number to text?"

"Yes," Elena said quickly. "I'm looking forward to it. Thanks," she said lamely.

"Elena," Dr. Steinhert said in a motherly tone, "I'm going to help you. You're going to be ok."

Elena felt a tear slip down her right cheek and she wiped it away quickly. "Thanks," she muttered under a sob. She didn't realize she had been bottling up all her emotions the past couple of weeks, but now it hit her like a giant wave, knocking her off her feet.

"I'll talk to you soon," Dr. Steinhert said sweetly. "Have a good weekend, Elena. Good-bye."

And that was it. Elena heard the buzzing tone that signified Dr. Steinhert had hung up the phone and she felt a sense of relief as she thought of her meeting coming up Thursday evening. She was anxious for the time to approach, and she wondered if things would get worse before they got better. She frowned as she considered this option.

Elena looked over at the clock on the stove. It was around 11:30 a.m. when she hung up with Dr. Steinhert. She pondered what to do with the rest of her day. Maybe she would try to call Mark or Frank's cell phone to let them know she reached out to Dr. Steinhert. She forgot to tell Hal that yesterday, or maybe she was subconsciously holding that information back from him. Either way – she didn't tell him, so right now no one knew that Elena was seeking professional help for her stress, and she figured Mark or Frank would feel relieved to know that she had called Dr. Steinhert. They would want to know that she was going to get better, right? she wondered. Then decided that yes, she should call them. But Mark was sick, she remembered. Maybe Frank would be better? But Elena felt more comfortable around Mark. Maybe she could just call him and leave a message for when he's better.

Elena held her phone in her hand, contemplating her options. She could keep the information about Dr. Steinhert to herself, she could relax today, or she could call Mark. After thinking through the different possibilities, she decided that telling Mark was the best thing to do. She wanted to ensure that the DOL knew she wouldn't fall apart with this project. She didn't want them to think her weak or unstable.

She unlocked her phone and went to Mark's contact info and called him.

She expected to get his voicemail, but surprisingly he picked up on the first ring.

"Oh, hello, Mark, this is Elena Brooks."

"Hi, Elena," Mark said in a raspy voice. He sounded weak, Elena thought. "Hal just told me he talked to you. Did you need something?" He paused. "I'm sorry about cancelling the conference this week. Unfortunately, I'm a little under the weather again." He coughed.

"Hal told me you couldn't talk," Elena admitted. "But I just wanted to give you an update – I called Dr. Steinhert." She stopped there.

"Um...well, that's it I guess," Elena continued when there was an awkward silence.

"Hal told you I couldn't talk?" Mark asked suddenly.

Elena was taken off guard by Mark's response, and then she recovered. "Yes, well he told me you were sick but when I asked if I could check in with you, he had said you weren't available to check in – you or Frank."

Elena could hear Mark tutting under his breath – she wasn't sure why. Then it became clear when he spoke again. "I wasn't aware that Hal told you this. I thought I had told him I was available to meet with you if you wished." He paused. Elena got the impression that Mark was annoyed.

"Well, I assume Hal just misunderstood," Elena said, trying to smooth things out before Mark got too agitated. She had only seen him get upset once before – when someone was caught sneaking off from the PS conferences and spreading rumors about the DEA project. He was furious. Elena had never seen someone get so mad, to be honest. And, she didn't want to ever hear Mark get that upset again. She hesitated before she spoke again.

"So, anyway...I just wanted to let you know I have a session with Dr. Steinhert this Thursday evening and we're going to get started with once-a-week sessions," Elena said.

There was a long silence. Then Mark sounded normal again. "That's great, Elena! I'm happy you reached out to her. I think she could be very helpful and I personally worked with her in my early days at the DOL – she was an amazing asset to my work."

Elena felt herself relax a bit. She didn't realize she was holding so much tension in her shoulders until she released them in that instant. She got up and walked over to the couch in the living room and sat down and leaned back. She rested her feet on the ottoman and crossed her legs, her slippers rubbing the fur against each other. She wriggled her toes quickly to let out a little anxious energy. "I'm glad to hear that," Elena said truthfully. "I was a little worried about starting therapy for the first time – I thought maybe you guys at the DOL would think less of me," she admitted sheepishly. "But obviously now I know that was a little silly of me," she stammered.

"It's not silly," Mark said. "It's completely understandable. You're used to doing everything on your own, not having a hard time succeeding in life – this is different for you. But you'll see, Dr. Steinhert will help you through this tough time."

Elena felt hopeful, truly hopeful, for the first time in weeks. It was like someone lit a fire inside her heart, giving her the extra energy she needed to move forward with this project.

"Thank you, Mark. And get some rest – we need you better

for next weekend's conference."

"Will do," he replied confidently. There was more life to his voice by the end of their conversation. Elena wondered if Mark had gotten lonely being home by himself sick the past week. "Bye," Mark said.

They hung up at the same time, and Elena threw her phone down on the couch as she stood up. She decided she would run to the grocery store soon and stock up on some much-needed food for her apartment. She grabbed her keys from the dish on the table by the door and headed out to her car.

Chapter 10

Thursday came before Elena could think much more about the DEA project. She didn't have any more sessions with Paige, but she had a couple of sessions with her other investigators throughout the week – Monday and Wednesday.

She received the text from Dr. Steinhert on Wednesday with the details of her appointment. There were no in-person doctor appointments anymore, but Elena hadn't been sure if her appointment would just be a phone call or a Zoom or Facetime session. The text message cleared that up –

Hi Elena, this is Dr. Steinhert, but you can call me Julia. I'm confirming your first appointment for tomorrow at 5:30pm. The session can be held over the phone or on Zoom, depending on your preference. Please respond back here to confirm your appointment and let me know if you would like to do an audio call or a Zoom call. Thanks!

Elena wasn't used to receiving long personalized texts from doctors. In the past, she had received the automated texts reminding her of her dentist appointments or her annual physical exam, but this seemed different. Somehow, it was like Dr. Steinhert – Julia – was reaching out a helping hand right when Elena needed it most. She promptly confirmed the appointment yesterday, opting for a Zoom video call over the audio call. She thought it might make the whole thing feel less uncomfortable for her. She was used to Facetiming with Jodi and her mom, so she thought she would feel better about divulging her inner demons if she could see the person she was talking to.

The clock struck 5:00 p.m. on Thursday and Elena was just laying around on the couch reading Harry Potter until it was time for her appointment. She wanted to not think about everything before she had to. Instead, she distracted herself with magic and adventures and problems that were not her own. But she couldn't help but wonder in the back of her mind what she and Julia would talk about for her first session.

She knew that she would be discussing the issues with work and Adam for the most part, but Elena wondered how Julia would get started. She knew all about building the therapeutic rapport from her classes in college, but somehow it seemed completely foreign to her when she was on the receiving end of the therapizing, as she liked to call it.

She watched the clock from 5:15 to 5:29, barely reading any of her book between glances. Then at 5:30, she logged onto her laptop and signed into the Zoom meeting that Julia had sent. There was a meeting ID and password and Elena quickly typed that in and got the message that the host would let her into the meeting when it started.

The waiting screen only stayed up for 30 seconds before Elena was admitted to the Zoom room and she saw Julia for the first time. Elena didn't know how she had pictured the woman looking, but she was definitely surprised to see that Julia looked as if she were at most 40 years old. She had assumed that since Julia worked with the DOL, that she had been working there since its inception, but then she realized, the DOL had only been founded in 2010. If Julia started her work at age 30, it would make sense that she's been working for the DOL for all ten years of its existence.

Julia had long, light brown hair with blonde highlights. It looked like she cared about her appearance very much, as not a single root was showing through the blonde streaks. Her makeup was done perfectly – a brown eyeshadow with thickly applied mascara, making her eyelashes stand out against her artificially suntanned skin.

Elena couldn't make out much below Julia's neckline, but she did notice a white collared shirt sticking out under a dark blue blazer. She was sleek and put together, like a china doll.

"Hello, Elena! It's good to virtually meet you," Julia said buoyantly.

"Hi," Elena responded. She sat up straight on the couch and crossed and uncrossed her legs, a nervous habit, as she waited to hear what Julia would say next.

"I know this is probably awkward for you," she said, "but I want to make this as comfortable as possible. I haven't talked to Mark yet because I would need you to sign a release form, but I figured if you want to do that, I can send that over after our session today. But for now, why don't you tell me a little about what's been going on."

"So..." Elena wished that she had written down her thoughts beforehand, that she had planned something to say, because now that the time had come for her to tell her story, she felt as if her mouth was glued shut. But she forced the words to come forward.

"This is my first special project with the Professional Students. I started back in May," she began. "I signed up to be a coordinator for the DEA project because I felt a strong connection to it because of the situation with my cousin Adam. I thought that doing something to help the college drug situation would make me feel better, but I'm realizing that as a coordinator, working with all the investigators and being invested in this project all the time, it's taking a toll on me," she stammered. "I'm stressed out. Things are getting hard because we're not making progress on the project, that is, until recently. We found out about a young woman who overdosed at one of my investigator's locations – she's ok, she'll live, but it shook me up a bit I think. It took me back to the other year with going through this all with my family, with Adam, and things turning out differently than they are now. Why is it that this woman gets to live, but Adam had to die?" she asked suddenly, as if that was on her mind the whole time, though she was just able to articulate it.

"Well, that was fast," Julia said. "Usually, it takes a few sessions to get to an epiphany like this, to come to an understanding about what's bothering you," she explained. "But I guess I shouldn't be surprised," she continued. "From what you told me about your background, you studied a lot of Psychology yourself. You're very in tune with your emotions," she said.

"I am?" Elena asked curiously. "I mean, I knew why I was getting stressed, but it just came to me now that the reason this is so upsetting is that some of these college kids are living, but Adam had to die. I guess I didn't have anyone to talk to about this until now. I couldn't talk about it with my mom or Jodi – my best friend – because I can't tell them about the DEA project. It's hard," she admitted solemnly.

They talked a bit more about how Elena was feeling. She dove into her sadness, her guilt, her resentment. Julia consoled her

– she did all the things Elena learned about in her own therapy courses, but Elena realized that this was actually making her feel better. Though she wasn't really uncovering anything new, it helped to just pour it out. She didn't realize how much she had been bottling up over the past couple of weeks.

The 45 minutes were up so quickly, Elena wondered if time had sped up. But they ended their session with Julia giving Elena some goals for this week. Elena was to keep a journal that she would write in each night, reflecting on anything she wanted to get out of her head that day.

Elena thought this sounded like an obvious idea – *why didn't I think of this myself?* But then again, this is why people seek professionals for this sort of thing. It's easier to spot problems as an outsider and to offer advice, rather than trying to solve your own problems inside your head. Elena truly believed this, and that was why she got into Psychology, but it really hit her in this moment to know that she could help others and still accept help for herself at the same time – it didn't make her weak – it made her human.

* * *

Elena spent the rest of her Thursday evening watching TV to decompress. They had covered some heavy topics in therapy today and she needed to do something fun. She put on a Hallmark Christmas movie on TV and laid on the couch with her pizza for dinner and zoned out. It's all the same plot, the Hallmark movies – the girl meets a guy, girl and guy get to know each other and fall in love on Christmas, the end – so Elena didn't need to pay too much attention to the movie to get the gist of it. She was having fun. She thought she might even give Jodi a call tonight. They hadn't talked in a week and Elena thought it would be nice to hear about her friend's holiday break, though Jodi had to stay on campus at NYU for the winter break as part of her teaching responsibilities.

Elena sent Jodi a quick text.

Hey. How's it going?

In no time at all, Elena received a reply:

Hey girl! Long time no talk. I'm good. Whatcha up to for the break?

Elena thought about how she would reply. She couldn't tell her about the therapy session because that would require her to say something about the special projects, but she could be as honest as possible.

Kind of having a hard time. Work is stressful. Wanna talk tonight?

There was a couple of minutes before Elena heard the ding of her phone signifying Jodi's response.

Sure! Give me a call whenever

Elena felt herself smile a true smile – she was going to talk to Jodi tonight and she was going to tell her some of what was going on, without revealing any of the confidential information. She flipped to Jodi's contact info and pressed the button for a Facetime call as soon as she finished reading her friend's response.

Jodi answered right away. She was sitting on her bed, laying on her stomach, her legs bent behind her, kicking back and forth with her bright red socks. "Hey!" she called out with a smile.

Then she looked a little more serious. "What's going on?"

Elena told her how there was a student in one of her classes who just overdosed and ended up in the hospital. She didn't tell her how this was related to her job, but instead just went forward by saying, "It just got me thinking about Adam. You know, I didn't really ever deal with that. My mom never talked to me about it, and I didn't talk to you much about it after it happened either – I didn't really talk to anyone."

"Yes," Jodi said consolingly. "I can't say I understand because something like this didn't happen to me or someone that I'm close to, so I don't think anyone can completely understand what you're going through right now, but I'm here for you. I'm here to listen if you want to talk and if you want advice, you know I'll offer some." She smiled at her friend, a sad, yet hopeful smile.

Elena smiled back, if not half-smiled. She appreciated Jodi. She was a great friend, and Elena wished she could disclose the full story about what was going on with her job, and in that moment, she felt so tempted to just screw confidentiality. She wanted her friend to be there for her completely, like she knew Jodi would.

Elena opened her mouth to start talking – she was so close to telling Jodi everything, but then she thought of her career and she stopped herself. She closed her mouth and simply nodded at Jodi, silently agreeing to accept her friend's advice and help, despite her not knowing the whole story.

"What is it, Elena?" Jodi asked. "Talk to me."

She knew, Elena thought. She knew something wasn't right. Elena didn't know how much longer she could lie to Jodi, but she would have to keep this up for the foreseeable future. Mark never told her if she could disclose any of the information after the special projects were completed. Elena wondered – would she have to permanently keep half her life a secret from nearly everyone who was close to her?

"It's just a lot," Elena said truthfully. "This job, the school

113

environment, being on my own with these memories – it's a lot to handle. I'm so glad you're here for me, Jodi, but I really wish you were *here* with me."

"I know, honey," Jodi said, sounding just like Elena's mom – caring, sweet, thoughtful, and invested in Elena's happiness. "It hasn't been easy for me either being on my own. I really do miss you. But we'll get through this – we always do, right?"

Elena nodded seriously, determined to keep a strong front up for herself and for Jodi. She couldn't fall apart, not now. "Thanks, Jodi," Elena said weakly.

The two women talked about some of the fun stuff they'd been doing in their spare time. Elena talked about rereading Harry Potter, as usual, trying to learn how to cook – and failing at it. Jodi talked about her writing – she was working on some poetry – something she'd never done before. One of her coworkers lent her a book by his favorite poet and Jodi fell in love with the art.

"Who's this friend?" Elena asked curiously.

Jodi blushed. "Just a guy I work with – Paul. He's really sweet and he's been working in the Psychology department for a couple of years now, but he was a Literature major in his undergrad, so he absolutely loves reading – you two would bet along great!" Jodi exclaimed.

"We've been hanging out and talking for about a month. And...well..." Jodi hesitated. "We're supposed to go out on a date next weekend at this Thai restaurant near campus. I'm actually super excited," she said.

Elena's jaw dropped. Jodi had only dated one guy seriously while they were at NYU together, and it had ended badly. Since then, Jodi hadn't dated, so Elena was so happy for her friend to be getting back out there.

Jodi talked for a little while longer about Paul, and Elena asked questions at all the right spots in the story, allowing her friend to expand upon the tales and give her all the details about her new "relationship."

After an hour or so of gossiping about Paul, Elena started to get tired. It was already 10:00. Elena had to wake up early tomorrow because tomorrow she was supposed to head over to the PS conference. Mark and Frank had called earlier today to let her know the conference was on for this weekend and Elena was excited to see her supervisors in person. She hadn't heard from Hal since their last conversation before last week's conference was cancelled, but Mark had mentioned that Hal would be at the conference this weekend.

She had to pack in the morning and then head out by noon to get to the hotel in time for her 2:30 appointment with Mark and Frank.

Chapter 11

The drive back to New York was uneventful. Elena spent the morning packing up her car because she would be going home for Christmas after the conference this weekend. She had to pack for a week and a half. Today was December 18th. She would be at the conference from the 18th - 20th and then she would drive home to her mom and dad's house for the holidays. She was excited to see her mom and dad, but she was also a little nervous about how she would navigate the topic of work without talking about the special project she was working on. She figured she should avoid the topic of the drug overdose altogether because Mom hated when she'd bring that up, but honestly, what else could she talk about? Maybe she'd have to broach the subject with her, feel her out to see how she reacts to Elena's newfound stress.

She was pulling into the hotel parking lot before she could completely think through how she was going to approach her mom. Her dad wasn't one to worry about – she didn't talk to him much anymore. With his new job, he was working long hours to try to support him and her Mom financially. As the General Manager at Food & Plate, Albert Brooks was a hard worker – always offering to stay later or cover for other employees, whether that be a manager, a cashier, or a box boy.

He loved his new job, but he was definitely overworked. As Elena thought about seeing her parents later this week, she felt a rush of emotion. She missed them terribly. As an only child, she had grown up with her folks acting as her best friends, but since graduating NYU, she hadn't seen them much at all. She had only been home to see them once since starting the new job in May – for Thanksgiving.

Elena shook herself out of her daze and got out of her black car. She slammed the door shut and hit the lock key twice on her keyring, not bothering to grab anything but her purse yet – she would come back for her bags after she checked in as usual.

They had her name down at the Marriot for her weekly conferences so she had her set room that she almost always stayed in. Today was no different.

"Room 104," the woman with the short, curly black hair and glasses said curtly when Elena checked-in at the front desk.

"Thanks, Barbara," Elena said with a smile to the woman she had been seeing nearly every week since she started her job at the DOL.

Elena went to her room, down the end of the long hallway next to the bar, and dropped off her purse. Then she ran back out to the car and got her bag for the next couple of days. She left the other suitcase in the back seat – that would be coming with her to her parents' house soon enough. She thought longingly of going back to Nesconset, entering their small, cozy, single-floor white house. She imagined staying in her old bedroom, where she had been living less than a year ago between when she graduated NYU and when she got the job at the DOL. It would be weird to be back there for a week. When she came home for Thanksgiving, she had to be back at the PS conference that weekend, so she only stayed for the day with her parents. This time was different – she wouldn't just come to the house for a home-cooked meal. Instead, she would be staying for a week of quality time with her family. While part of Elena was looking forward to this, she couldn't help but feel torn between longing to see her family and the urge to get back to her own place and remain independent.

When Elena returned to her hotel room, she was still thinking about her trip home. She deposited her small suitcase with her business attire on the floor next to the dresser and the television. She pulled out her suit and hung it up in the closet quickly, before it could get too wrinkled – she hated ironing so she wanted to avoid that at all costs. She held up the hanger with the suit in front of the mirror and examined it. It didn't look bad, she thought, though she could use a new suit for Christmas. She did tell her mom that was the only thing she really wanted this year, but she knew her mother would surprise her with a couple of other small gifts. Elena wished she wouldn't – she wished her mom and dad would save their money instead of buying her Christmas gifts she didn't need, but she assumed, that's part of being a parent. The feeling that you need to provide things for your children that they don't necessarily need, even if it puts you behind to get those things.

Elena went all out for Christmas this year. She finally had the money to afford nice gifts for her mom and dad, so she splurged on a new slow-cooker and purse for her mom, and a gift certificate for a year of landscaping for her dad. It was starting to get too hard for him to maintain their lawn in the spring with all his work.

Elena left the gifts in the trunk of her car, but she thought of them sitting there, wrapped in the Christmas wrapping paper and in the festive card, and she smiled to herself. They were going to love the gifts, she was sure of it.

Before she could fully emerge from her daydreaming about giving her parents her gifts, there was a knock on her door.

Elena wasn't expecting anyone. She looked at her watch – she wasn't late for her meeting with Mark and Frank. She walked to the door and looked through the peephole and saw Hal standing there, his hair brushed down neatly and his black suit gleaming in the light of the hallway.

Elena unlocked the door at once. "Hi, Hal," she said. "Do you need me for something?" she asked curiously.

"Hi, Elena," Hal greeted her with a friendly smile. "Just wanted to stop by to give you a message from Mark and Frank – they wanted me to let you know they're running a little late, so if you could come to their office at 3:00 p.m. instead of 2:30, they would really appreciate it."

"Oh, thanks," Elena said uncertainly. "Is everything ok?"

"Yes, of course," Hal said. "Just administrative business, or at least that's what they told me," he said in a tone that Elena may have only imagined was a bit annoyed. Elena knew there was some tension between Mark and Hal, especially since her last phone call with Mark when she told him that Hal had said not to call him. She wondered if he confronted Hal about this. And then, she wondered if Mark told Hal that Elena had ratted him out – was Hal annoyed with her? She didn't want to get Hal on her bad side, although he didn't seem to be a major player in the DEA project as of late.

Hal looked over Elena's shoulder, expectantly. "Anyone here with you?" he asked. Elena looked into Hal's blue eyes – they were blaring at her, daring her to defy him.

"Um, no," Elena said uncomfortably. "Just me, as usual," she said. She wondered who Hal was expecting.

"Well," Hal said in a much more friendly tone, "would you want to grab a drink with me at the bar while you wait for Mark and Frank? It's only 2:15 now, so you have 45 minutes." He smiled in a way that made Elena question his intentions. She did notice in that moment that Hal looked rather younger than she first thought. He was probably in his mid-forties. But still, Elena thought, he couldn't be hitting on me, right? He wouldn't try to make a move with one of his subordinates. Though, Elena thought, he got moved off of her project, and she wondered if this had anything to do with that. Did Hal want to get closer to Elena? She felt suddenly uncomfortable, like she was walking through a sheet of ice.

"You know, I'm kind of tired. I think I'll take a nap before I meet with Mark and Frank." She let out a long fake yawn. "Long drive," she explained shortly. "I'll see you later!" Then she closed the door gently before he could ask again. She knew that look – that was the look of yearning. Hal had expected Elena to say she would have a drink with him – he had wanted to be alone with her. She twirled a piece of her hair around her pointer finger, thinking. But Elena never thought of Hal that way. She never once thought of him as anything more than a supervisor. She was a little skeeved out by it to be honest. She wasn't one to date someone twice her age, though she thought, Hal wasn't exactly twice her age – but he was probably close. Not like Mark, she thought, who was definitely around her age. Then she shook that thought too. No, she thought, I don't like Hal or Mark that way. And, I don't want to ruin my chances with advancing at this job. Definitely not, I cannot go on a date with one of my supervisors. I need to get a grip, she thought.

She walked back toward the bed shaking her head, her mind bursting with thoughts and questions. Was this why Hal hired her? Was Elena only a Professional Student because Hal was attracted to her? If she turned him down, would this cost her, her job? But that couldn't be – Mark and Frank had been the ones to choose her for the coordinator position. Hal hired her initially, but it was Mark who got to know her. He knew she belonged here – didn't he? But then Elena thought of Mark and she felt a pang of guilt. She knew she had some sort of feelings for Mark. She had gotten to know him very well over the past few months, and she trusted him more than she trusted anyone really. She couldn't do this. She couldn't fall into the trap of the young love on the job – she wouldn't turn into a cliché.

Now she really needed a nap to clear her head. She laid down on the bed in her sweats and decided that she would set an alarm for a half hour, then get up and change before her meeting. She wanted to look professional. As soon as her head hit the pillow and she closed her eyes, she barely had a chance to set the alarm on her phone and then she was out like a light.

* * *

Elena woke up to the loud ringing of her alarm on her phone. She quickly rolled over, suddenly wide awake and refreshed, and hit the stop button. She promptly hopped out of bed and walked over to her duffel bag where she found a pair of tan khakis and a black button-down shirt that were folded neatly on top. She changed into her business casual attire in the bathroom, threw on a little makeup, grabbed her purse, and then exited the room at top speed. She should be at her meeting in exactly one minute. She had cut it rather close with her nap, but she could still make it in time – their office was right down the hall. It was like the nap had erased all the negative thoughts nagging at her. She didn't think about Hal at all as she walked toward Mark and Frank's office at a brisk pace.

As Elena approached the office door with the plaque on the outside that said "Business Room 1," she looked down at her watch and saw the second hand just passing the 11 – she was right on time. She knocked two times on the door, and before she could take a second to smooth out her shirt, the door was opening before her and Mark was standing in the doorway expectantly.

"Hi, Elena," Mark said softly. "Frank is just on a phone call, but he'll be off in a minute. Come on in," he said as he gestured through the door toward the chair in front of his desk. She saw Frank at his desk on the phone and she could hear a few words coming from his end of the room "Yes, sir...saw it with my own eyes...yes, I understand...yes..." Frank looked up and waved at Elena, as Mark walked her over to his desk on the other side of the room. She took her seat as usual and Mark sat across from her in his tall cushioned chair behind the desk.

"So, let's get started," Mark said. "I know Hal told me you had some news, and he shared that with me the other day, but I wanted to hear it from you, because...well, between you and me, Hal probably won't be working on this case much longer. His temporary reassignment just became permanent." Did Mark look jealous, Elena wondered? It was as if talking about Hal was bringing up a side of Mark that Elena had never seen before.

"Oh," Elena said uncomfortably. "Is there any particular reason?" she asked curiously.

"It was an administrative decision," Mark said simply. He did not look like he was about to divulge any more information about the matter, so Elena let it go. Yet she wondered what was going on.

She went on to tell him about her conversation with Paige, trying not to leave out any details. After she told him about Sarah's condition, she went on to explain that she had in fact been very stressed lately, and that as she told him on the phone, she called Julia Steinhert and she'd had her first session with her.

"Yes, she gave me a call after your session. You filled out a release form, I presume?"

"Yes," Elena said. "I sent it back that evening, so I figured she would talk to you at some point, but I didn't think she would have talked to you that same night."

"Julia is very meticulous with her clients. She likes to do her due diligence, especially at the start of a new case," he explained. "Trust me," he said, "you're in good hands. And of course, I had nothing but good things to say about you." He smiled a genuine smile – he wasn't just trying to be nice, she thought.

"Alright, you guys, I'm ready to get started," Frank called over from his desk, hanging up the phone with a sigh of relief. "Long call – very boring to tell you the truth."

"Well, we're just finishing up here, Frank. Is there anything specific you needed to talk to Elena about?" Mark asked distractedly, rustling through a pile of papers in the top drawer.

"No, I think you can catch me up, right, Mark?" Frank responded.

"Of course," Mark said quickly, pulling out a couple of papers from the pile he was going through. "Here they are!" he said holding up the papers.

"Sorry," he said sheepishly. "I've been searching for these receipts for office supplies for the past week with no luck 'til now."

Elena looked down at her hands in her lap, uncomfortably.

She wondered if she should mention anything about Hal asking her out. She didn't feel comfortable with the idea of Hal trying something again, but then again, she didn't want to ruin her chances at advancement with her career. Maybe she misinterpreted what he was asking, she thought. Maybe he was really just trying to be nice – nothing more. She felt that she couldn't accuse him of anything...yet. She would have to just keep her guard up, she decided, standing up and waving goodbye to Mark and Hal. She went back to her room, and she chanced a look at the bar before she went to her door – Hal was indeed at the bar having a drink, alone. Elena felt a little sorry for him in that moment – it was like he had no friends at the DOL. She had thought when she started that Mark and Hal were really close, but it seems that since starting work on the DEA project, Mark and Frank had developed a bond that sort of left Hal out. And, all that administrative stuff with Hal moving around assignments – it seemed like everything was in flux at the DOL right now. Elena hoped that this didn't mean she had to worry about her own job.

She turned away from the bar, her hair flipping behind her as she did so. She reached the door of her hotel room and decided she would spend the rest of the evening going through some of her notes before the official conference started in the morning. She would have her one-on-one sessions with her investigators tomorrow to look forward to, when she might learn any new details that could help with the case.

Elena pulled on her cozy PJs, made a cup of decaf coffee, and laid down in bed with her folder full of notes from all her sessions. She turned on the TV to a mindless baking show, lowered the volume so it was just low, dull white noise in the background, and got to work.

* * *

The next morning, Elena awoke before her alarm could go off at 6:30. She must have fallen asleep early she realized as she looked around at the loose papers on the bed, her pen and notepad laying by her side. The blanket was disheveled, as if she had been tossing and turning all night, though she felt like she'd slept rather soundly. She made a pot of coffee in the room before she had even fully woken up. She needed the caffeine to prepare her for today. It was definitely going to be a long one, she thought. Though she didn't dread working at the conferences exactly, she wasn't looking forward to running back-to-back one on one sessions with all her investigators in one afternoon. It was enough to exhaust anyone.

Elena quickly showered and got herself dressed in her suit, put on some makeup, and grabbed her stuff to bring down to the conference room for breakfast and opening remarks. She was supposed to meet Paige and Patrick by the breakfast buffet at 7:15. It was now 7:05. Elena figured she would head down a few minutes early and get a good seat towards the front of the room with the other coordinators – unfortunately she couldn't sit with Paige and Patrick during the opening session because the coordinators had to be together at a table with the supervisors, Mark and Frank.

Elena put her bag down at the table at the front of the room next to the podium and the projector screen then sprinted to the coffee table. She always followed Paige's initial advice – you had to get the fresh coffee by the front of the lobby. She took a sip and she was in heaven. Finally, fully waking up, she spotted Paige and Patrick walking into the lobby towards her. Paige's black dress nicely contrasted against her pink cardigan, but kind

PROFESSIONAL STUDENT

of clashed with Patrick's red button-down. The couple were holding hands and smiling and waving at Elena from across the room.

"Hey," Paige greeted her, reaching out to hug Elena carefully, without spilling her coffee. Patrick held out his right hand stiffly. "Hello," he said. It looked like he was forcing a smile, but then again, Elena had always been closer to Paige than to Patrick. She thought Patrick might still be holding a bit of a grudge against her for dragging Paige into this special project. He didn't seem too enthused by the idea of going undercover for the DEA, and Elena could understand that.

The three of them stood in the lobby. Paige and Patrick got their coffee and they hovered in the corner by the door to the conference room, chatting happily. Paige was telling Elena all about the vacation she and Patrick were going on in the spring. They were each taking a week and a half off from work to go on a cruise to the Caribbean in March. They'd booked the trip this week.

Elena didn't want to spoil their fun by bringing up work-related conversation now – they had plenty of time for that throughout the conference events – so she continued to listen to Paige and Patrick tell her all about the excursions they were planning and the different islands they'd be visiting. They hadn't gone on a vacation together yet – even though they'd been dating for three years. Neither of them had time, between school and work, so they were really looking forward to this getaway to relax.

Suddenly, Elena heard the microphone static, indicating that someone was about to speak.

"Testing, testing," said Frank in his deep voice.

"We'd better get to our seats," Elena suggested.

126

They carried their plates they had made from the breakfast buffet to their respective tables and sat down quietly. All eyes were on Frank.

"Happy Holidays, everyone!" Frank said joyfully. "We almost made it through the year. And boy, has it been a long one. I really appreciate all your hard work on our project, and without further ado, I'm going to turn this over to your supervisor, Mark Sampson."

There was polite applause as Mark stood up from Elena's table and switched places with Frank at the podium.

He had a clicker in his hand. When he held it up, the projector screen went on. The slideshow read

"Professional Students 2021 – DEA Project 05481 in Review"

Mark cleared his throat. "As the year comes to a close and another semester ends, it is time that we reflect upon the progress we have made with project 05481..."

He went on to describe all the information Elena already knew – that the drug overdoses were occurring in an unlikely population – college students who had no history of bad behavior whatsoever. That the most recent overdose had occurred at the University of Southern California. That they hadn't come closer to discovering who was behind the drug dealing, but the project coordinators had made excellent progress working with all of the investigators to collaborate regarding all the details of their experiences on campus.

Then Mark's tone changed. "Now, I would like to make an administrative announcement."

He paused and gestured toward Hal, who had suddenly appeared at the table behind Elena.

"Hal has been promoted to Financial Manager of the DOL. This means that he will no longer be overseeing the Professional

Student program and he will no longer be a point of contact for you on a daily basis." He paused and smiled.

"I'd like to take a moment to congratulate Hal on his promotion and I know that we all wish him well. Would you like to say anything, Hal?"

Hal approached the podium hesitantly. He took the microphone that Mark offered him, and said, "Thank you everyone," as the polite applause started to die out. "I have enjoyed every moment of working with the Professional Student program and I will miss all of you. Just know, that if you ever need someone at the DOL to lend an ear, I'm still around and willing to help and listen. Thank you!" he said simply and walked back to the table.

There was more polite applause.

Mark returned to the podium. "Now, let's all break up into our groups." He gestured towards Elena's table. "Coordinators, you know which rooms to go to. You may begin," and then he walked away towards Hal and Frank. They were in the corner talking quietly while Elena, Thomas, George, and Hannah raised their hands, calling over their investigators to follow them to their breakout sessions.

Elena led the way to Meeting Room 3, where she usually went, and her group of investigators followed, Paige in the front of the crowd, walking beside Elena. When they reached the room, the investigators gathered around the sign-up sheet hanging on the wall. They each picked a time slot for their individual session with Elena, who now sat at the front of the room, ready to answer any questions that the PSs had during this time. There were a few questions about the protocol for the winter break. Another PS asked Elena if there was any pattern associated with the drug busts so far? Did the students have anything else in common besides what Mark talked about with them being "good kids?" Elena answered as best as she could, based on the information she had. Then the crowd started clearing out. They were heading back to their rooms for their break before their individual meetings. Elena let out a sigh of relief – she checked the sign-up board and saw that her next meeting was in 20 minutes. She had time to run back out to the lobby and grab another cup of coffee before it started.

As she was pouring her coffee, she could hear Frank and Mark talking, their backs turned to her.

"Yeah, he's not really happy about it for some reason," Mark said quietly to Frank, who raised his eyebrows in surprise.

"Financial Manager? That's a huge promotion, at least regarding pay. I'd be thrilled if I actually had the finance background!" Frank exclaimed.

"I know," Mark said. "But I know Hal. He doesn't want that. He's not in this for the pay raise. He wants to be out there making a difference, so in a way I get it. He's going to be working behind a desk now..."

Elena quickly walked away with her coffee, hoping that Mark and Frank didn't realize she'd overheard their conversation. She went back to her meeting room and started her check-in with Heather.

She went down the list of all the investigators, but in the back of her mind, she was thinking about Hal – was he really unhappy with his promotion? She couldn't help but feel sorry for him if he was.

The rest of the day passed in a blur and the remainder of the conference was uneventful. By Sunday evening, Elena was more than ready to get out of there and head to her parents' house in Nesconset for the holidays. All the Professional Students were getting a little stir crazy towards the end of the conference. Even Paige and Patrick rushed out as soon as they could, barely stopping to hug Elena goodbye and wish her happy holidays.

But no matter – Elena was so excited to see her mom and dad that she didn't even worry any more about Hal as she drove off towards her childhood home, Christmas presents waiting in the trunk to be opened in the days to come.

Chapter 12

The house was just as Elena had left it. She walked in the front door, with the Christmas wreath hanging on the front, and wiped her feet on the "Joy to the World" doormat.

"Hello?" she called out as she closed the front door behind her.

Her mom's car was out front, but her dad's was not. She wondered if they were both out this Sunday night.

"Elena, in here!" her mom called from the kitchen. "I saved you dinner," she said, rushing out to hug her daughter. Mary Brooks and her daughter looked almost exactly alike – they could have been sisters. Both small, lanky, baby doll face – the only difference was the glasses. Elena's were large and thick black-rimmed, while her mom's were thin wire frames.

The two women embraced for a long minute, before Mary held her daughter back at arm's length to take a look at her. "You're looking a little frail," she said with a frown. "Come on, eat up. I made lasagna."

Elena took her mom's hands off her shoulder and walked to the kitchen counter with a smile. She grabbed a plate from the cabinet above the dishwasher and served herself a large helping of her mom's meat lasagna – her childhood favorite.

As Elena stuffed her face, her mom watched and told her

about how her dad was stuck working late tonight. There was a problem at the store and they were open late for their holiday hours. Elena listened, slightly disappointed that she wouldn't see her dad tonight. She was planning on turning in early to get some extra rest. She wanted to start talking to her mom tonight about what was going on, but she looked so happy to see her daughter, and she was so concerned about her getting enough sleep, that Elena didn't bother staying up and sparking a conversation tonight.

The women said their goodnights and Mary walked Elena up to her room, helping her carry her bags that she brought in with her clothes for the week and the Christmas gifts. When Elena reached her room, she hugged her mom one more time, took her bags and dropped everything inside the doorway. She pulled her comfy flannel PJs out of her suitcase and changed quickly before grabbing her book and hopping into bed. She kept on just the nightstand lamp. Before she started reading, she looked around at her room – not a thing had changed. Same light purple walls, same wooden dresser, same dark, sturdy desk in the corner where she always did her schoolwork. It was like she'd never left. For a minute, she forgot about all the stress she had been experiencing with work and wondered what it would be like to just move back home.

Elena didn't read more than a couple of pages of her book before she trailed off to sleep, dreaming of moving home. She was working as a therapist in her local town, living down the street from her parents – an easy small-town life without all the major stressors she had been experiencing as of late. Elena slept so soundly, dreaming of a quiet life, and when she awoke, she felt like a new person.

She sat up in bed and thought about her dreams, and then

realized, as good as that sounded, she knew it wasn't what she was meant to do. She was meant to be a Professional Student. She was meant to work for the DOL, she decided. She would have to work through her stress, and that meant being as honest as she could be with the people she cared about, including her mom.

She was determined to start a serious conversation with her today, as she got ready in her room. She was putting her glasses on and brushing her hair before she went downstairs for breakfast. She could smell French toast – she knew her mother was a little worried about her, and when Mom was worried, she cooked.

Elena's slippered feet hit the bottom step leading to the first floor of the house, and she immediately saw her mom in the kitchen, standing over her French toast bake, slicing it and serving a piece on a plate, holding it out toward Elena when she saw her approach.

"Thanks, Mom," Elena said gratefully as she took the plate. Her mom handed her a cup of black coffee and placed the container of syrup on the table. Elena sat down and started eating and drinking – she was suddenly starving, and the coffee was really perking her up. She hadn't realized she was still half asleep until the warm roast of the Pat's coffee hit the back of her throat and invigorated her.

"So," Mary said, "what's on the agenda for today?" She looked expectantly at Elena, as if Elena had her whole trip planned out.

"What do you mean?" Elena asked. "I don't have an agenda," she laughed.

"Well, what do you want to do?" her mom proceeded to ask. "We can go shopping, go for a walk, go out to eat – whatever you want."

Elena considered her options, then said, "How about we go for a hike, like we used to? At Avalon?"

"Oh yes!" her Mom said excitedly. "That sounds wonderful. It's a little warmer out today – high of 40 – so I think we'll be ok outside for a long hike."

Elena felt relieved. She knew Avalon would be rather quiet during the winter, and she hoped she could talk to her mom in peace as they hiked today. It would be relaxing, yet somehow, she was stressed out at the thought of broaching the subject of drugs with her mother. She didn't know how she'd react.

After breakfast, the women got changed into thick leggings, boots, and a sweatshirt. They pulled their hair back into matching ponytails so they looked even more like sisters. Then they threw on their winter coats and hats, put their gloves in their pocket, and packed a drawstring bag with water and snacks. They were ready to leave for Avalon by 11:00. It was only a 20-minute drive from their house, so they'd be out on the trail before noon.

The drive was uneventful. They talked about the weather and the holidays approaching. "Can you believe Christmas is in just four days?" Elena's mom asked.

"I know," Elena said. "I feel like Thanksgiving was just the other day. It's nice to be back," she said happily, smiling wide.

Elena was waiting until they started hiking to bring up the topic she really wanted to talk about. She thought her mom might be more receptive to talking while they were doing another activity, but she wasn't entirely sure. When they got to Avalon, they set off down the blue trail – the shorter of the three trails – saying that they could loop around again if they felt like it.

"My classes this semester were great," Elena said enthusiastically. "I really loved the professor, Dr. Likert. She seemed to like me too – said I could be a really good Psychologist someday, that I had a way with understanding people and getting them to talk."

Elena's mom looked at her daughter and smiled. "I'm so glad. I know you wanted to go to an Ivy League school when you were applying to colleges yourself, so I'm so excited you get the chance to study at Yale now, as part of your career." She squeezed Elena's hand in both her own. "You're just doing so much great work – it's inspiring, honey, really. You're going to be able to live a comfortable lifestyle at the rate you're going... " she trailed off. Elena could hear a hint of resentment in her voice. She wondered if her mom was a little jealous – jealous that Elena had this whole career ahead of her, while Mom had to give up her own career when she was injured. She never talked about it with Elena, but now that she thought about it, Elena felt stupid for never asking her about it before.

"Do you miss it, Mom?" Elena asked sincerely. "Nursing?"

Her mom's smile faltered. "Well, yes, I certainly miss it. Some days I wish that I could just go back with a bad back, but I know the doctor will never clear me. Hiking is one thing – lifting patients is another. But at least I have your father, and you of course." She forced a grin.

They made their way through the woods and around to the red path. "You know, Mom, there is something I kind of wanted to talk to you about..."

"Of course!" her mom said instantly. "Anything!" She looked at Elena expectantly.

"Someone in one of my classes overdosed on drugs suddenly," she stammered. She just had to get it out. Her mom's face fell

135

drastically.

"That's — terrible," her mom said, choking out the words. Elena could tell she wished she could take it back. She didn't want to make her mother uncomfortable, but she pressed on — she couldn't keep lying to her about something so important in her life.

"Yes," Elena continued, "it is terrible. And it's making me think a lot about Adam," she said, keeping her eyes off her mom. She didn't know what to expect next.

"I think we should talk about something else," her mom said stoically. Then it looked like she reconsidered. "Well, actually — what do you want to know?"

"I don't exactly want to *know* anything exactly. It's more that I just want to talk about how I'm feeling," she explained. "This person lived — the person who overdosed in my class. And it just got me feeling really mad, I guess. Like why did Adam have to die, but this young woman got to live? It just seems so unfair," Elena said, sniffling back a few tears. It was all starting to hit her now and she didn't know what to do about it.

Elena's mom stopped walking. She put her arm out to stop Elena, too. "I only want to say this once, and then I don't want to talk about it anymore, ok?"

Elena nodded solemnly.

"What happened to Adam was a tragedy. And I know we never talked about it, and I'm sorry about that — but you know Aunt Trish didn't want anyone spreading rumors about what happened," she said. "But I know you were close with Adam, and I want you to know that it's not your fault he died — there's nothing you could have done. It's unfortunate, but there's no rhyme or reason to this kind of stuff. It's a sad accident. What happened with your classmate was also a sad accident — it just ended differently." She stopped suddenly and looked into Elena's eyes, tears forming behind her own. "I'm sorry," she said finally.

Elena reached out to hug her mom and she cried. She wished so badly that her mom would talk more to her about Adam. She felt like she needed to get more out about it, but she supposed that talking to Julia would help. She would have to rely on the professional for this, she thought.

The women talked about mindless topics for the rest of the hike. They even took the long yellow trail around once in silence. But it didn't feel uncomfortable, somehow. Somehow it felt safe. Elena knew that her mom knew how she was feeling and that was enough right now. She had been heard.

They drove back to the house and relaxed for the rest of the day, reading and watching Hallmark Christmas movies late into the night. They continued their Christmas movie marathon for the next few days, right up until Christmas morning, when they stopped to celebrate and exchange their gifts.

Elena's father was home for Christmas Eve and Christmas Day, so she got to spend some time with him. On Christmas morning, she pranced down the stairs with her small pile of gifts for her mom and dad, and greeted them both in the den, merrily.

Her dad was sitting in the armchair, facing the TV, but reading a book, as per usual. His beady blue eyes were reflected in his round glasses. His book was half read – another mystery by his favorite author, Yen Hallard. Albert Brooks was wearing his red plaid pajamas and his fluffy grey slippers, his legs crossed, looking comfortable, relaxed, yet wide awake.

"Hi sweetie," he said to Elena as she appeared.

"Merry Christmas, Dad!" she said as she handed him his card

with the gift certificate. "Merry Christmas, Mom!" she handed her mom the purse and the slow cooker, wrapped in the red and green paper – she hoped they would be a pleasant surprise.

As her dad opened the card and read it, Elena's Mom ripped the paper from her purse and proceeded to "ooh" and "ahh" for the next few minutes, holding the purse at arm's length, studying it from every angle. "I love it!" she gushed.

"Oh, and this is great!" her dad said suddenly. She looked back to see him holding up the landscaping gift certificate with a wide grin plastered across his face. "It's perfect for the spring," he said. "Thank you so much!"

Elena's mom opened the other gift and smiled. "So now I can cook you more food when you come to visit since you can't cook for yourself?" she laughed.

"I love it," she said truthfully, standing up from the couch to walk over and hug her daughter.

"Now it's your turn," Elena's mom said conspiratorially, a smirk on her face, her eyes gleaming.

She walked to the Christmas tree and took out the large box that was sitting under it – the lone gift left there – and handed it to Elena.

"From us," her mom said, standing over Elena's dad with her arms around his neck.

Elena smiled and ripped the gold paper, trying not to make too much of a mess. There was tissue paper inside the box too. She unwrapped the tissue and saw that she had a brand-new black pantsuit and a pink shell to go underneath the blazer.

This was a designer suit – it must have cost a fortune, Elena thought. She looked at her mom and dad and wanted to say, "it's too much," but when she saw how happy they looked giving her the gift, she changed her mind. "Thank you! I love it!" she said honestly.

She hugged them both, one arm each. Then her mom walked into the kitchen to turn the music on the Alexa. They played Christmas carols and ate the pancakes her mom had made earlier, and just sat in each other's company and enjoyed the day. Elena thought, she almost forgot about how sad and stressed she had been the other day. How could she be upset on a day like this? She had a family that loved her and she loved them very much as well. What more could she want?

She decided that she would get a little more rest the day after Christmas before heading back to her apartment in New Haven and get ready for her next semester of classes, and of course, more DEA work. There was always work to be done with the Professional Student organization, but, she thought, that could wait a couple of days. Now was her time with her family.

Chapter 13

The drive home dragged out. Elena was excited to be going back to work, but she couldn't help feel a little disappointed that her vacation was coming to an end and she worried that she would get overly stressed again. She had her one-on-one with Paige that evening, so she wanted to get back to her apartment and unpack first.

She unlocked the door of her apartment, walked inside with her two suitcases, and dropped them both by the couch. She was wearing her comfy sweats, but she would have to do her hair before her Zoom call with Paige – she had to at least pretend to act professional. Elena unpacked her things, throwing most of the clothes back in her closet because she did a load of laundry at her parents' house, and sauntered to the bathroom with her makeup bag in hand. She emerged from the bathroom 15 minutes later with her face and hair looking considerably better than before. Her hair was straightened and down past her shoulders and her light makeup accentuated her eyes and lips, without making her look like she was going out to a club.

When it came time to call Paige, Elena sat at her desk in her room, opened her laptop, and placed a notepad and pen next to her in case she needed to take quick notes. She always preferred writing her notes to typing them – it just made them sink in better. She opened up the DOL Microsoft Teams meeting and waited patiently for Paige to arrive – it was 5:58 p.m. and their meeting was scheduled for 6:00.

Paige's dark brown hair was curly today, and her red lipstick stood out against her porcelain face. She looked like she had seen a ghost.

"I have to talk to you," Paige said shortly.

"Um...ok, isn't that what we're doing now?" Elena asked. "What's going on?" she asked after she saw Paige squirm on the screen.

"I think I know something about the DEA project. I didn't want to tell you before break, because...well, I didn't want to ruin anyone's holidays, and I wasn't really sure if it was anything serious, but now that I've had the week to think about it, I think it's worth mentioning," she rambled.

Paige looked into Elena's eyes, silently pleading for her not to blame her. "I think I saw a couple of people trading drugs outside my class before break," she said quickly. "And they were talking about trading something else – they didn't call them drugs, but I know what I saw – now I'm sure of that."

"Paige," Elena prompted her friend, "is there anything else you saw or heard? I mean, this is big news, and I wish you told me sooner, but I'm happy that you're telling me now and I'm hoping we can act on this information."

"I tried to get a little closer to the two people, but I think they saw me inching towards them. I looked away and when I turned back around to find them, they were gone," Paige said nervously. "I'm kind of scared, Elena. What if they think I'm going to rat them out? Because, I mean, I am ratting them out. So, what does that mean for me?" She sounded lost.

"We'll figure this out," Elena said with more confidence than she felt. "I just have to reach out to Mark and Frank and we'll figure out where to go from here," she explained calmly.

Elena's mind was racing. Was her friend in trouble? Elena knew only too well that when drugs were involved, people made rash decisions. Look at Adam, she thought. But she didn't want to go there. She couldn't go there...

She would just have to wait until her session with Julia on Monday, though she didn't know how she could hold on for another two days with this knowledge.

"I have to go," Paige said suddenly. "Patrick's coming, and he doesn't know any of this – I don't want him to get dragged into this," she said desperately.

"It's fine," Elena said. "Go. I'll call Mark and Frank right after we hang up and we'll come up with a plan."

They both hung up at the same time, and Elena frantically flipped to Mark's contact info to call him. The phone rang four times and then went to his voicemail – but it was full. Not discouraged, Elena called Frank instead. The phone rang five times and then went to his voicemail. She left a message. She didn't want to disclose too much on the voicemail though – Frank and Mark always taught her to be wary of the security of technology. She thought about what to say and then she heard the beep signifying the start of her message.

"Hi, Frank. It's Elena Brooks. I have some information about project 05481. I received a new lead from Paige Andrews and I wanted to talk to you and Mark about it to determine next steps. I tried to call Mark, but his voicemail was full. Um...I guess just please give me a call back as soon as you can – it's kind of urgent. Thanks."

Elena was on edge – she didn't know what she was supposed to do until she received a call back from one of her supervisors, but she decided on just reviewing her notes until she could talk to Julia. She was feeling extremely overwhelmed now – what Paige told her had her very worried about her friend, and she thought she knew why, but she couldn't put it into words on her own.

She decided to turn into bed early, though she wasn't sure if she'd be able to sleep with so much on her mind. However, she did find that her head was pounding, threatening to burst with everything she knew – so maybe her body would welcome a good night's sleep.

She took two 3-mg melatonin pills just in case and made a cup of tea to bring to bed with her. She got ready for bed, laid down with her tea and her book, and turned off all the lights in the apartment except for the lamp on her nightstand. She plugged her phone in to charge and then decided to put on some soft music. She flipped to her favorite station on Pandora and lowered the volume so it was barely audible – just enough to calm her down before she could fall asleep.

By the time Elena finished her cup of tea, she could feel the melatonin kicking in. Her eyelids were heavy and despite all the thoughts still swirling around in her head, she felt that she could relax enough to sleep. She left the music on, but closed her book and put it aside on her bed, rolled onto her left side, closed her eyes, and waited for sleep to overcome her.

* * *

Sunday came and went without a call from Frank, and Elena was starting to get more nervous. But then, Monday morning approached and she had her session with Julia to look forward to, hoping that this would alleviate some of her worries.

At 9:58, Elena sat down at her desk with her laptop, opened Zoom, and entered the waiting room. Julia admitted her to the Zoom room at exactly 10:00. Julia was smiling, until she saw Elena's pale, scared face and her smile disappeared.

"What's wrong?" she asked suddenly.

"It's Paige," she said. Then she went on to explain what happened with her one-on-one with Paige – the talk of the drug deal, them seeing her, Elena calling her supervisors to no avail – it just all came pouring out. Before she knew it she was crying over the Zoom conference, but Julia stayed put together. She looked stern, yet concerned.

"So your supervisors didn't call back yet then? You haven't heard from them?" she asked hopefully.

"No, I have no idea where they are – they always answer the coordinators' calls...except – I completely forgot!" she exclaimed. "They told me they were going to a three-day conference after the holidays. I don't remember the dates but I'd bet anything that's where they are. It's some sort of mandatory DEA training in Ohio and they said they'd have limited access to phones and computers. Ugh!" Elena yelled. "This is just great – terrible timing – terrible!"

"Ok, I understand it's bad timing," Julia said. "But what can we do about it? Why do you feel like this is so terrible to leave until they call you back?"

Elena pondered that question, biting her thumb nail as she thought. She thought she knew the reason, but she really didn't want to say it. But she had to, right? How would she make progress with her career and her mental health if she wasn't honest with her therapist?

"My cousin, Adam. He didn't die from the overdose," she said bluntly. "He committed suicide a week later, after he recovered from the overdose, physically at least," she explained. "I know that people with drug problems can make rash decisions – they might not be thinking clearly. So what if these guys that saw Paige take matters into their own hands and try to stop her from telling the truth? What if they hurt her?" She started to cry.

Soon, Elena was sobbing uncontrollably. "I can't lose another person who I love! I can't go through that again!" She smacked her thigh with her left palm in frustration.

"Elena," Julia said. "Listen to me."

They made eye contact for a minute.

"This isn't the same thing that happened to Adam. But I understand how you feel. What do you think you need to do to make things right?" she asked curiously.

"I...I...I think I need to go to Paige," Elena said at last. "I need to go to the University of Southern California and see what's going on for myself. Maybe I can keep her safe until Mark and Frank return my calls."

Julia smiled. "I think," she said, "that is a very rational decision."

"You do?" Elena asked. "You don't think I'm being irrational?"

"No," Julia said. "I think you're worried about your friend and your career is on the line – you have to do something. I'm not going to tell you what to do, but I think you're making a good choice. Just follow through with it," she advised.

"Thanks, Julia," Elena said gratefully. "I've gotta go. I need to book a flight," she said confidently.

Elena clicked the leave button to end the Zoom meeting. Then she slammed her laptop shut, packed it up in its case, and grabbed her phone. She went on the Southwest Airlines website and found the next flight to San Diego. She booked the flight for early the next morning – 5:30 a.m. – she would drive to LaGuardia airport from New Haven and take that flight to San Diego, get to Paige by 9:00 a.m. (California time) and start making headway on the project. She didn't feel prepared exactly, but she knew what she had to do.

She packed her bag – she wasn't sure how long she'd be staying in California, so she packed a few outfits and the essentials – and got ready for bed, being sure to set an alarm for 1:00 a.m. to give her time to drive to the airport. It was only noon, Monday. She had time, she thought. She would look over her notes for the next couple of hours, try to call Frank and Mark again, and then call it a night – she would definitely have an early start.

She laid in bed with her book, the room light out and the nightstand lamp the only source of light, and she tried to relax, tried to calm her mind. But she couldn't. She ended up tossing and turning until midnight and then she fell asleep for an hour before she had to wake up to head to the airport. She was absolutely exhausted, but she made her coffee and put it in a to-go cup and hit the road by 1:30 a.m.

Chapter 14

The airport was deserted when Elena parked her car and made her way to the entrance. There were only a few cars in the visitor lot, short-term parking, and when she stepped inside, she passed only one woman who also looked like she was trying to catch an early flight.

Elena's bag was small enough to be a carry-on, so she didn't have luggage to check. She went through security quickly – there was no line. And was waiting by gate 13 at 4:30 a.m. She had an hour to kill before her flight. She couldn't think of anything to do but pace back and forth. Instead, she settled on buying a coffee and a muffin from the stand by the gate. She just realized she hadn't eaten anything since breakfast before her therapy appointment.

She thought about calling Paige to let her know she was coming, but she didn't want to worry her. She would wait until she landed in San Diego to call her. Elena was planning on taking an Uber to Paige's school anyway, so it's not like she needed Paige to be aware of when she arrived at the airport.

"Now boarding Flight 2221," the announcer said.

That was Elena's flight. She picked up her bag and looked down at her ticket, B15 – they would board the A's first, then the B's. She would be boarding towards the middle. She didn't care though – as long as she made it to San Diego as soon as possible.

"A's 1-30," the woman behind the stand called out. "A's 1-30, line up here," she said, gesturing to the first line. After a few minutes, the woman called A's 31-60. After a few more minutes it was time for B's 1-30, so Elena ran over to the line and took her position. She was ready to board and she didn't want to waste any time. She handed her ticket to the flight attendant at the stand by the door, and walked through to the plane. The plane was about half full when she got on, so she walked to the first available seat, the front in the middle. She didn't care where she sat, to be honest. She put her bag in the upper compartment.

"Excuse me," she said politely to the man in the aisle seat. He stood up so she could squeeze through to the middle seat. She got settled with her earbuds, plugged them into the armrest, and watched the TV before her. It was a movie channel that was on the screen to start. She flipped through a few stations until she found the last of the Hallmark winter movies and settled on that. She leaned back, crossed her feet, and put her arms on the armrests and tried to relax for the six-hour flight.

The flight seemed to drag on and on. Had it really only been an hour? Elena thought to herself at 6:30 a.m. She could have sworn it had been at least three. But she knew she was anxious to get to San Diego. She figured she should probably come up with her plan while she was on the plane.

First, she thought, she would take an Uber to the University of Southern California. Then, she would call Paige and let her know she was there. There would be nothing Paige could do to stop her from coming by the time she was already on campus, she thought. She knew Paige didn't tell Patrick about what was going on, and she didn't want to expose the situation for her, so she decided she would try to meet Paige outside of their apartment, so Patrick wouldn't hear what they were up to. Maybe a coffee shop on campus?

Then, she would have Paige show her the place where she had witnessed the drug deal and ask her more questions. She was sure that she would come up with more things to ask when the time came – this was what Dr. Likert had seen in her – an ability to ask questions and probe people to find out what was going on. Oh, and she would try to call Frank and Mark again when her plane landed. So far, no luck with them. It still went straight to voicemail and Elena tried to remember when the conference would be over for them so she could get a better idea of when they'd respond, but no matter how hard she racked her brain, she couldn't remember.

No matter, she thought. She would handle this on her own, at least as much of it she was capable of on her own. She and Paige made a good team – they could make some progress on their own.

By the time Elena had her plan all settled, the plane was landing in San Diego.

"Please fasten your seatbelts. We are beginning our descent," the flight attendant announced suddenly. Elena hadn't unbuckled her seatbelt at all on the trip, so she just remained seated for the next 5-10 minutes until the plane landed smoothly on the runway.

"Welcome to San Diego, California," the friendly flight attendant said after the plan came to a stop. "Please take all your belongings with you as you exit the plane."

Elena would be one of the first people off the plane because she was sitting in the front row. She waited for the man in the aisle seat to grab his things, and then she stepped out of the seat and took her bag from the overhead compartment and made her way out of the aircraft. She was speed walking through the airport, trying to find the exit to the Uber pickup area.

She quickly pulled out her phone and booked an Uber to pick her up in a couple of minutes and take her to the University of Southern California. It couldn't come fast enough.

She stepped outside the airport and saw the silver Hyundai Sonata waiting by the curb. She rushed over to the car. The man opened the window and said, "Elena?"

"Yes, that's me," she responded urgently.

She opened the back door and got in with her bag.

"University of Southern California, San Diego?" he asked, bored.

"Yes, please," she said.

"Should take about 15 minutes," he said.

Elena tapped her foot on the ground to the beat of the music until they pulled up in front of the University of Southern California gates that marked the front entrance.

"Here is good," Elena instructed the driver, pointing to the sidewalk by the gate.

He pulled over and said, "Have a nice day!"

She jumped out of the car with her bag and swiftly walked up the sidewalk path to the main building, pulling out her phone as she walked. She dialed Paige's number and waited for her friend to answer. "Please pick up, Paige..." Elena prayed.

"Hello," a sleepy voice answered.

"Paige?! It's Elena."

"Elena? Why are you calling so early? It's only like 7:00 a.m.?" She sounded half asleep.

"I'm here," she said simply.

"You're what?" Paige sounded much more awake now.

"I'm here. At the University of Southern California. I came to see you. I needed to hear more about what was going on with the drug deals, and I was worried about you. I wanted to help," she explained.

"Elena, you shouldn't have come," Paige said seriously. "This is my mess to be in. I don't want to drag you into it..."

"I'm the coordinator. It's my job," Elena said with more confidence than she felt in that moment.

"Ok, well, where do you want me to meet you?" Paige asked.

"I know you're not telling Patrick about what's going on, so let's meet outside of your apartment," Elena said calmly. "How about a coffee shop? Is there one nearby?"

"Sure," Paige said. "Right by the administrative building, there's a Starbucks," she told her.

"Great. I'll meet you there in about 10 minutes," Elena said quietly.

Elena pulled out a map of the campus on her phone and followed the path to the administrative building. Then she went around the right side of the building to the Starbucks entrance.

Paige was outside the door, arms crossed, looking critical of Elena.

"Why did you come here?!" Paige rounded on her as soon as she got close enough. Paige pushed Elena's shoulder in a half joking, half serious sort of way. "You weren't supposed to leave New Haven. You were just supposed to send Mark or Frank!"

"They wouldn't answer my calls," Elena said. "And besides, I wasn't going to leave you here by yourself after you told me that those two guys knew you saw them trading drugs. No way – I don't trust them," Elena said emphatically, shaking her head furiously.

"Ok, well what are you going to do?" Paige asked seriously. "We can't exactly take on a few bigger guys in combat or something…"

"I know," Elena said. "We just need to buy us time for Mark and Frank to get here. But I have to be honest with you, Paige. There's a reason I'm so invested in this special project – there's a reason I wanted to be the coordinator and there's a reason I'm here now."

She hesitated – did she want Paige to know about Adam? She hadn't told everyone about him and she hadn't talked to anyone besides Julia about his suicide. But she had to explain to Paige – Paige deserved to know why Elena was so concerned. "My cousin, Adam, overdosed on drugs a couple of years ago. He died – but not from the drugs, or…not directly. He committed suicide after he physically recovered from the overdose – couldn't handle what had happened to him. That's why I'm so invested in this project. And that's why I couldn't leave you here knowing that those guys saw you watching them make a drug trade. Drugs make people do crazy things – and I didn't want anything to happen to you! You're one of my best friends," she said in a rush of emotion.

"Elena," Paige began quietly, "I had no idea you had such a personal connection to this case. Do Mark and Frank know?"

"Mark knows," she said. "He urged me to talk to that psychologist on staff, Julia Steinhert, and I finally made the call before the holidays and set up a couple of appointments. Don't worry about me, though," Elena said seriously. "I'm here for *you*. We have to make progress on this case, or at least stop anyone from messing anything up before Mark and Frank can get here."

"Well why don't I show you the spot where I saw the people making the trade?" Paige suggested.

"Sure. By the way, how did you happen to come across them while they were trading?"

"I figured out what they were doing after class," Paige explained. "I kept hearing them talk about trading Shadows, and at first I thought it was some kind of game, but then the more I heard the context it was being used in, the more I realized something was up..."

Elena was only half listening to the rest of what Paige said. "Did you say 'Shadows'?" Elena asked curiously.

"Yeah, I think that's what they called them," Paige said. "Why?"

"It sounds familiar...I think I heard someone at Yale talking about them too."

"That makes sense!" Paige said excitedly. "Remember what I told you about the girl, Sarah, who overdosed here? She started acting weird after she came back from visiting her sister at Yale. I wonder if this is connected somehow."

"We're going to have to tell Mark and Frank about this as soon as possible," Elena said seriously. "But I don't know when they're going to start answering or returning calls again..."

Elena and Paige went into the coffee shop at last, and sat down and tried to talk about other things. They tried to not think about what was going on with the Professional Student program, but each woman could tell that the other was worried.

"I just don't want Patrick to worry either," Paige said at last. "I don't want him to know that we got ourselves in this deep. This is the last thing he wanted to happen."

"We'll keep it to ourselves then," Elena said. "Can I stay with you for the night? I can tell Patrick that I just came to visit for the break. We can say we have something planned for all day tomorrow and then hopefully we can get this all settled with Mark and Frank by the end of the day and then Patrick won't have to worry at all."

"Sounds too good to be true," Paige said woefully. "I just don't know how we're going to pull this off, Elena. I feel like we need to do some digging. Maybe we should go bring our laptops to a study room in the library and search through any articles that have been posted about the drug ring in colleges? Maybe we can uncover some sort of clue based on what we already know."

"I don't know…" Elena said uncertainly. "Maybe we should wait for Mark and Frank?"

"We can't just sit here and do nothing!" Paige said angrily.

"You're right, you're right. Let's go and try to make some progress."

The two women picked up their things and made their way toward the library. It was completely deserted and when they checked in at the front desk, the librarian told them all the study rooms were available. They could take their pick.

"Thanks," Paige said.

They walked up the stairs to the second floor where the study rooms were. Most of them had glass windows so you could see inside them from out in the library, but Paige and Elena opted for a more secluded, private room in the corner, without glass walls. They didn't want anyone to find out what they were up to, though really who was going to be searching around the library for a couple of undercover DEA investigators? Elena thought.

The women hunkered down at the table in the study room, took out their laptops, spread out all of Elena's coordinator notes and got to work. It was going to be a long day, they thought.

* * *

By the end of the day, Elena and Paige hadn't made much progress. They did find that there was a connection between the start of the drug overdoses and Yale, though they had spread throughout the country, the women found that there was always a connection to Yale – whether it be where the person's friend went to school, or where they had visited family.

They felt like this was a solid piece of evidence they could bring to Mark and Frank, but when they called again, they still got Frank's voicemail.

"I think the conference ends tomorrow," Paige said. "I remember them mentioning the dates at one point a couple of weeks ago at our weekly check-ins."

It was getting late, and Elena and Paige didn't think they could stare at their notes any longer for the day. They decided to call it a night, grab dinner on the way back to Elena's apartment and watch a movie before they went to bed. Hopefully in the morning, Mark and Frank would return their calls.

Chapter 15

Elena woke up on Paige's couch to a door slamming. She opened her eyes and saw Paige running around the apartment, opening and closing doors. "He's not here," she said, scared.

"What?" Elena asked sleepily. "Who?"

"Patrick, of course! He was supposed to come home late last night and we must have fallen asleep, but when I woke up a little while ago, I noticed he was gone, and his phone is on my nightstand. He doesn't do this. He doesn't leave without telling me..."

Elena perked up instantly. "You don't think anything happened to him?" she asked.

"I don't know. What if he overheard some of what I was talking about?" she asked frantically. "What if he tried to find out more information on his own?"

"Has he been asking a lot of questions about what you're up to with the project?"

"Now that I think about it, yes," Paige said. "He's always asking me if we have any leads and what me and you discuss in our sessions. I thought he was just trying to protect me, but what if there's more to it?"

"We have to find him," Elena said. "Let's check his phone and see if he had any missed calls or texts. Do you know his password?"

"Yeah, 0213, our anniversary," she said stoically. "I'll get his phone." Paige rushed into the bedroom and returned promptly with Patrick's iPhone in her hands. She was already trying to unlock it when she reached Elena.

"He just has texts from me, his parents, and a couple of his buddies...but wait, here's a missed call. Wait a minute, I recognize that number," Paige said. "That's Hal's DOL office number!"

"Maybe he was calling for Mark and Frank. Maybe they were trying to reach us," Elena said hopefully.

"Maybe..." But Paige didn't sound so sure.

"To be honest," Paige said, "I've had a bad feeling about Hal. Something about him just rubs me the wrong way. And, he kind of made a pass at me one weekend when I went to the conference without Patrick. He asked me to meet him at the bar for a drink, out of nowhere," she explained.

"He asked me out too!" Elena exclaimed. "I feel like this is more than just a coincidence."

"There's a voicemail!" Paige said suddenly. "Let's listen."

Paige played the voicemail on speaker phone and they both heard Hal's voice as if he were standing there with them:

"Hi, Patrick. This is Hal, from the DOL. I have some information about the DEA project, specifically about Paige. Can you meet me at the Coffeehouse on 25A in San Diego tonight? I don't want to say too much on the phone – I don't trust that people aren't listening. Give me a call back, or just meet me there at 8:00 p.m. – thanks!"

He sounded friendly enough, Elena thought. But this was weird, why was Hal calling Patrick about Paige? What kind of information could he have?

"This isn't right," Paige said. "Something's up. We need to go to the Coffeehouse on 25A and see if we can retrace their steps."

"Let's go," Elena said, already making her way towards the front door. Paige grabbed her keys from the kitchen counter and they made their way toward the parking lot to her car.

Paige drove them to the Coffeehouse at top speed. When they arrived, they knew they were going to have to do some digging to figure out where Hal and Patrick went. Obviously, they weren't going to still be at the Coffeehouse the next day, but maybe they could find a clue as to where they went next.

Then they noticed Patrick's car parked in the back of the lot of the Coffeehouse. That was definitely his blue Toyota Corolla. Paige and Elena saw it at the same time and they looked at each other, nervous.

Then, Elena and Paige barged in the door, panicked, looking frantically around for any hint of Patrick. Finally, they decided to ask the barista if she had seen Patrick and Hal.

"Hi, I was just wondering if you were working last night?" Elena asked the barista sweetly.

"Yes, actually I was closing the place last night. I'm the manager. Can I help you?" the tall brunette, named Lisa, according to her nametag, said.

"Well, Lisa," Paige began. "I'm looking for someone. He's missing, in a sense. We think he was here last night with another man. Their names are Patrick and Hal. Patrick is about my age, a few inches taller than me, with glasses and messy brown hair. The other man, Hal, is much taller and bigger, with shaved brown hair. Do you think you could tell us if you saw them last night?" Paige asked hopefully.

Lisa closed her eyes as if deep in thought. "Yes," she said

suddenly. Then she pointed to the far-right corner. "They were sitting at the table over there. They were here for maybe 30 minutes and then I heard the bigger guy, Hal?, yelling a little. Well maybe not yelling, but definitely raising his voice. It seemed like they had gotten into a bit of a fight, and then Hal stormed off, leaving Patrick sitting at the table alone. The young man, Patrick?, he sat at the table with his coffee for another hour or so before heading out."

"But we noticed his car outside. Are you sure he left alone?" Paige asked.

"Certainly," Lisa said nodding. "There was no one else here when he left, though now that I think about it, I did notice a truck parked out front for a good portion of the night..."

"Was it a red pickup?" Elena asked suddenly.

"Yeah, I think so," Lisa said, thinking hard. "Does that mean something to you?"

"Yes, thank you, Lisa. You've been very helpful," Elena said. Then she gestured for Paige to follow her outside.

"That was Hal's pickup," she said quietly. "I've seen him drive it before. It's his spare car."

"So, do you think Hal was waiting for Patrick to leave the Coffeehouse?" Paige asked, frightened.

"It's the only lead we've got..." Elena started to say until her phone vibrated in her pocket. She looked at the caller ID and saw that it was Mark.

She answered right away.

"Mark!? Oh boy have we got a lot to tell you. I'm with Paige now, and we have a lead," she started to say, until Mark cut her off.

"We've solved the case," Mark said excitedly. "The DEA Project – Hal's solved it!"

"Hal!?" Elena and Paige both said, as they were leaning over the phone to hear what Mark had to say.

"Yes, I'll explain everything when you get back to headquarters. We're having a ceremony tonight."

"But, Mark, we have a problem," Paige said, grabbing the phone away from Elena. "Hi, Mark, it's Paige. Patrick is missing and Hal is the last person he was seen with."

"That can't be right," Mark said seriously. "Hal has been here all week. He was working at his new position when he got an anonymous tip about a drug deal going down at Yale. That's how he figured it out! I can't explain everything over the phone, but you need to get back here, ASAP."

"Mark – are you not listening!? Patrick disappeared with Hal last night and never came home. Hal left him a weird message on his phone telling him to meet him at a coffeehouse because he had information about me. I don't know what's going on, but something isn't right with Hal. You need to hold off this ceremony and help us find Patrick!"

Elena stood by her friend's side and listened as she screamed at her supervisor. Elena was ready to back Paige up, when Mark got quiet.

"Now that I think about it – Hal did have an awful lot of information in a short period of time. He said he got one tip and then he did some digging on his own, but..."

Now Elena grabbed the phone. "I think Patrick knew something. Paige said he's been asking her a lot of questions lately about the project and her work with me – what if Patrick had the information that Hal received."

"Ok," Mark said. "But then, why wouldn't Hal just bring Patrick back to the headquarters and relay the information. Unless..."

160

Mark paused. Then suddenly – "I think I know what's going on. You have to get back here quickly and help me investigate – both of you."

"We'll get on the first flight," Elena said at once.

* * *

Their plane landed at 4:00 p.m. EST in New York. Mark was waiting for them at the airport. Elena and Paige spotted him and walked right over. They all got in the car, Mark in the driver's seat and they were on the road before Paige and Elena could even buckle their seatbelts.

"Where are we going?" Elena asked Mark.

"The police station," he said simply. "I think that's where Patrick is."

"Why would Patrick be at the police station?" Paige asked frantically.

"I think Hal had him arrested."

"What!?" both women yelled.

"Let me explain," Mark said. "Hal told me the story of how he had an anonymous tip about a drug ring at Yale. He said he was calling from headquarters, that he had followed up on the lead, arrested one of the culprits, but the other had gotten away. At the time, I was so happy we made progress on the case that I didn't question anything he said, but..."

"Elena, this is important," Mark said suddenly. "Do you remember Dr. Likert at Yale?"

"Of course," Elena said. "She was my professor this past semester. What does she have to do with this?"

"Hal told me she was one of the people pushing the drugs on the students at Yale. She may have even been the leader of the whole thing. He said he interrogated one of the drug dealers – the one he locked up – and he confessed. But what if the 'drug dealer' was Patrick?"

Paige and Elena looked at Mark curiously.

"Patrick isn't a drug dealer!" Paige yelled adamantly.

"I know that," Mark said. "Stay with me here – I think Hal is framing Patrick. I think Patrick is the one who gave him the information about Dr. Likert. I have a hunch that we're going to find him at the police station, and we need to try to hear his side of the story."

They were pulling into the police station before Elena and Paige could think more about this crazy scheme.

When they arrived, Mark flashed his badge at the officer and said he needed to see the holding cell – anyone who was taken there last night or this morning.

The officer, though seemingly confused, obliged. He led the three of them back to the holding room, down a dark, quiet hallway.

When they opened the door, Elena and Paige's jaws dropped. Patrick was sitting at the table with a bunch of thugs, crying.

Paige ran to him. "Patrick! You're ok!"

"Paige!? Elena, Mark!? How did you find me? Wait – did Hal send you here – you can't believe him, you just can't. He just wants to solve this case. I think it has something to do with his job. He kept mumbling 'my job's safe now. They'll see!'"

Mark all of a sudden stomped his foot. They all looked at him strangely. "I've got it," Mark said.

"But first, we need to get you out of here, Patrick."

Mark explained that he needed a professional courtesy to let Patrick be released into his custody.

"Fine by me – he's a whiner anyway, that one," the officer

muttered.

All four of them got back in Mark's car and then he floored it back to headquarters.

When they arrived, Mark jumped out of the car ahead of the other three and told them to follow him.

He led them back towards his office, and when they entered, they saw Hal, seemingly celebrating with his boss, Bill DeBlase.

They were toasting champagne when Mark pointed at Hal and in an accusatory tone, said, "You didn't solve this case!"

Bill DeBlase, wearing his new blue suit with the light blue tie and a puzzled expression, turned to Mark. "Um, Mark, we were just celebrating Hal's success. Please, join us," he said uncomfortably.

"Sure, I'll join you, but not to celebrate Hal," Mark said. Then Patrick stepped into view and Hal's face dropped.

"Patrick?" Hal asked confused. Then he composed himself and turned to DeBlase. "Sir, this young man was one of the drug dealers that confessed. I arrested him and I have no idea why he's here with Mark. He needs to go back to the station immediately," he instructed calmly, though Elena could tell he looked uncomfortable.

"Sir," Mark said. "I know this is going to come as a shock, but Hal didn't solve this case. He framed this young man so that he could take his information and pass it off as his own."

"It's true, Mr. DeBlase," Patrick said stepping forward confidently.

Then Patrick went on to explain the whole story. How he had figured out what was going on with the drug ring on his own. That he was just about to tell Paige he needed to go back to headquarters to report on something, when he got the strange call from Hal.

After he went to meet him, Hal tried to convince him to work together to solve the case together, but Patrick said he wanted to go to Mark and Frank on his own.

Hal got angry and stormed off, or so Patrick thought. When he exited the coffeehouse an hour later, Hal cornered him in the parking lot and handcuffed him.

"I was completely taken off guard. I had no idea what was going on," Patrick explained.

"But then I knew that Hal was trying to take credit for solving the case."

Everyone stared at Hal, in disbelief.

"Is this true?" DeBlase asked Hal seriously.

Hal collapsed down into the chair and raised his hands in defeat.

"I can't do this anymore," Hal said finally.

"After you told me I was off the case, I took matters into my own hands," Hal said. "I just didn't want to lose my job – it's my life – I couldn't just sit idly behind a desk pushing papers for the rest of my career," he tried to explain. "I bugged Elena's phone. I had been listening in on her and Paige's one-on-ones and I knew they had a lead. I had a hunch that if I came out to San Diego, I'd be able to find out more. When I got there, I found Paige and Elena at the coffeeshop on campus, but I also saw Patrick hovering in the corner, watching them. I knew he knew something, so I decided to make my move. I thought maybe I could get him to cooperate with me and I could get credit for solving the case on my own, but once I realized that wasn't going to happen, I had to figure out another way of getting him out of the way."

"But, Hal," Mark said. "Why did it have to come to this?"

"This was going to be my last assignment on the Professional

Student program," Hal said, his hands forming fists at his sides – he was shaking with anger.

"I can't do that. I have to work. This is my life – you know that, Mark," he said quickly. "I'm sorry," he said honestly. "I didn't mean for it to come to this. I didn't mean to sabotage the project, but I didn't know what else to do. I couldn't lose my life, not yet."

"Hal," DeBlase said, "what did you do?"

"I don't know," Hal admitted softly. "I made a mess out of things – that's what I did, and I don't know how to make it right."

"You're fired," DeBlase said simply. "So don't even try to make it right."

DeBlase turned to Mark, Elena, Paige, and Patrick. "What do we need to do now?" he asked. "Hal said the professor, Dr. Likert, got away – how are we going to find her and stop her from starting another conspiracy in the colleges?"

"Well, I might not have been completely honest about that..." Hal said. "I wanted to solve the case completely so I was waiting for right before the ceremony to call the Dean of Yale and turn Dr. Likert in. I didn't get a chance to do that yet. I didn't want to make it look too easy," he explained.

"We're going to have to call the Dean of Yale to try to get to the bottom of this," Mark said.

DeBlase and Mark ran out of the room to get to the office phone.

After a few minutes of talking – Elena only heard Mark's side of the conversation, but it didn't sound good – Mark hung up the phone dejectedly.

"She's definitely gone," he said to DeBlase.

"That was the Dean. Apparently no more than two hours ago,

Dr. Likert notified the Dean that she was going on a sabbatical. She didn't give a date of return, but promised to reach out within the month."

"Good luck with that," said Hal.

Mark glared at him, with eyes that could kill.

"I hope you're happy," DeBlase said to Hal. "Now this operation is going to keep going on, but you're done working for the DOL. I want your badge, now," he said, pointing down at the desk in front of him.

"I'm sorry," Hal said truthfully. Then he reached into his pocket and pulled out his ID card and badge and gently placed them on the desk before him.

In no more than five minutes, a group of Professional Students entered the building and followed the chaos to find Hal, Mark, DeBlase, Elena, Paige, and Patrick. Mark quickly cuffed Hal and brought him into a holding room.

Hal didn't put up a fight.

The Professional Students watched the scene in awe. Their former supervisor was being led away in handcuffs. Elena imagined Mark and DeBlase were going to have a lot of explaining to do.

The gang was all there, waiting for what to do next, but no one knew what to do.

Mark instructed everyone to head out to the main conference room – that he would be making an important announcement.

As everyone filed into the room and took their seats, Mark stood at the front of the room, smoothing down his tie, thinking of what he was about to say to everyone.

Elena walked up to Mark, and in that moment, he looked so much younger than she had ever seen him. He was scared – that much was clear. His face looked not a day over 30, though

Elena had never noticed this before. She cleared her throat to get his attention.

"What are you going to say to everyone?" Elena asked curiously.

"The truth," Mark said. "You all deserve to know what happened today and you all deserve to know what kind of man Hal really is."

"You know," Elena said to Mark. "Paige and I had a bad feeling about him recently. He was hitting on us, or so we thought. I'm thinking now he was just trying to get more information out of us. But if either of us had told you what we were thinking and feeling – I mean – is this our fault for not acting on our instincts?" she asked desperately.

"No," Mark said. "You cannot blame yourself for this. Hal has problems. He made a lot of poor decisions and that isn't your fault or Paige's fault, so just forget about that." He paused. "I have to make this announcement," he said, gesturing at the crowd. "Please, sit down and we can talk after."

Elena, Paige, and Patrick had to sit through the whole story again, though this time, hearing it beginning to end, it seemed to make so much more sense. Everyone seemed shocked that Hal would do such a thing, but Elena and Paige looked at each other knowingly – they'd had a hunch about this, and they didn't act on it.

After the ceremony, Mark approached Elena.

"Um, Elena," Mark started. "Can I talk to you for a minute?"

"Sure, is everything ok?" she asked.

Mark began to walk away from the crowd and Elena followed him, intently.

"Would you like to go out with me sometime?" he asked in a rush of emotion.

Elena was shocked. Was this a test? She opened and closed her mouth, but no sound came out.

"I'm sorry," Mark said. "I know this probably isn't the time, but I like you – a lot – and I've been thinking about this for a while and now that Hal's out of the DOL, I'm going to be taking his new position. So that means..."

"You won't be my boss anymore," Elena said, finally comprehending where this was coming from.

"Yes, I've wanted to ask you out for a while now, but I knew it was against protocol because I was your supervisor. But, as the Financial Officer, I would be overseeing completely different parts of the DOL. And I'm not trying to hide this from anyone," he stammered. "I already talked to DeBlase. I wanted to make sure I wasn't doing anything out of order," he explained.

"You talked to DeBlase about asking me out before you talked to me?" Elena asked incredulously.

"Well, yes," Mark said. "But only because I needed to make sure I wasn't breaking any rules!"

Elena laughed. "Oh, Mark, I wouldn't expect anything less from you. You've always been doing things right by the book since I started here. And I'd be lying if I said I didn't think about you at all in this way." She looked him in the eyes and smiled widely. "Ok, let's do it," she said. "I'd like to get to know you outside of work," she said.

Mark leaned in toward Elena and kissed her, gently yet Elena could tell, with passion. She was taken off guard, but she wasn't displeased. He pulled back, and said, "Sorry, I shouldn't have done that," blushing beet red.

Elena reached out for his right hand and leaned back in and kissed him back, quickly. "Don't be sorry," she said with a smirk.

They spent the remainder of the evening talking at headquarters, Paige and Patrick away from them watching curiously.

They all reconvened after all the other Professional Students left the building. They were happy, yet when they made eye contact with one another, and relived the events of the evening, they grew serious, and sad.

"What do we do now?" Paige asked. "Do we all still have jobs? Or is the Professional Student program over?"

"Why would it be over?" Mark asked surprised.

"Well," Elena said, "now that you're not running the show and Hal is gone – who's in charge of our program?"

Mark smiled knowingly. "I think I have someone in mind."

Mark called DeBlase over toward them.

"Sir," Mark said, "I'd like to recommend Miss Elena Brooks to be the new supervisor of the Professional Student program. And I suspect, she will want Paige to be her partner?" he asked, looking at the two of them conspiratorially.

"Yes!" Elena yelled, hugging her friend, and new partner.

"Well," DeBlase said, "I guess I don't have much of a choice now do I? You ladies did an excellent job with this case and if Mark trusts you both with the program, then I do too!"

* * *

The next day, Elena and Paige were working together on plans for the Professional Student program. After some training from Mark and DeBlase, they knew that they needed to recruit more PSs and come up with new special projects for them to work on. They also still needed to work on tracking down Dr. Likert, but no one had heard anything from her.

They sent out an alert to all the nation's universities, with a description of Dr. Likert, so they would know not to hire her. They thought it might just be a matter of time before she turned up again.

And then, a week later, Elena received a phone call from NYU.

"Ms. Brooks?" the woman on the phone greeted her.

"Yes, this is she," Elena said. "Is there something I can help you with?"

"This is Dean Arthurs of NYU. I've had a suspicious candidate interview for one of our Psychology professor positions, and I think this might have something to do with the Dr. Likert person you warned us all about. She had different colored hair, but I think this is the woman you alerted the universities about. Can you come down here and check it out? We didn't want to confront her so the staff just told her we'd give her a call back with our decision about the job by this weekend."

Elena was practically jumping out of her skin with excitement. This was the first real break they'd had with Dr. Likert since the other week when everything went down at the DOL. Elena waved over Paige, who was sitting at her official-looking desk on the other side of the office.

Elena explained everything to her partner and they decided they needed to take a trip to NYU sooner rather than later.

When they arrived at the administration building of NYU, Dean Arthurs was waiting by the door for them. She was expecting them.

"Thank you for coming so quickly," Dean Arthurs said.

"It's no problem," Elena said. Paige nodded in agreement.

"Well, we did what you said. We called her back for a second round of interviews and she should be arriving shortly. You're sure you have enough staff to handle her?" Dean Arthurs asked hesitantly, looking at the two small women before her without backup.

"We've got it," Elena said simply.

As if on cue, Dr. Likert, or Dr. Bennett, as she was being referred to now, walked through the doors and saw Elena. Dr. Likert hadn't known Elena was working for the DEA, so she didn't think anything was wrong. But then, Elena walked right up to Dr. Likert and said, "That's her," to Paige. Then Elena flashed her badge, and Paige came behind her with handcuffs.

"Dr. Likert, you're under arrest for allegedly running a student drug ring at colleges across the country..."

"This is absurd," Dr. Likert said. "My name is Dr. Bennett."

"The jig is up, Dr. Likert," Elena said confidently. "I was in your classes at Yale. I remember you. And I was helping with the DEA project. You're busted," she said triumphantly.

As Elena and Paige led Dr. Likert away from the building and to the cop car parked out front, they exchanged a celebratory high-five.

They had solved their first case together. But what was going to happen now? Elena thought. Would everything change now that she'd solved her first special project? Would her other projects be as dangerous as this one? Could she finally disclose some information to her mom and Jodi?

There were more questions than answers at this point. But the two women just walked back to Elena's black Honda, hopped in, and Elena drove them home. They were sharing an apartment in Hauppauge now, right up the road from headquarters.

While a lot had unfolded over the past week, Elena wouldn't change any of it. She finally got to make a difference. She finally got to do something to remember Adam and feel like she was helping others like him.

Elena and Paige's apartment came into view as they pulled

into the complex. They opened the white door, and dropped down onto the sofa in the living room, right in front of the TV. It had been a long couple of weeks, and the two of them were enjoying the rest of the day off. They deserved it, Elena thought.

Then Elena's phone vibrated in her pocket and when she checked the caller ID, she saw that it was Mark.

She was expecting his call. He knew they were at the tail end of the project and Elena was sure he wanted to celebrate.

"Hi!" Elena answered the phone happily. "I'm assuming you heard?" she asked him.

"Yes! Congratulations!" he said. Though he sounded distracted. "Um, Elena, I'm actually calling because we have another special project for the Professional Students to get started with."

"Why are you letting me know?" Elena said, not unkindly.

"Well, we kind of have a personal connection to this case...

"Apparently, Hal's admitting to more crimes while he had worked at the DOL, but he refused to divulge all the details. We need you to work with the other Professional Students to find out exactly what happened. Something about stealing money from the DEA..."

"Shit," Elena said at once. Paige looked up from the TV.

"Everything ok?" she asked.

"Ugh, I'll have to explain this assignment to Paige," Elena told Mark quietly.

"Thanks for letting me know though," she said. "Bye."

Elena explained the situation, or the little that she knew about it, to Paige and they started working on a plan. They would have to strategize. They started listing the different Professional Students that Hal worked with in the past and realized that a few of them had quit after Hal was fired. Elena originally thought this was because they were so distraught about the loss of their mentor, but now she wondered if they hadn't been hiding something.

They had to track them down. But this was a project for another day, she thought. Today, she was taking a well-deserved break with Paige and they could resume their daily tasks tomorrow.

Elena, sitting back on the sofa next to Paige, leaned back and propped her feet up on the small coffee table. She crossed and uncrossed her legs, her gray fluffy slippers sticking out like a sore thumb as usual, and decided that this was definitely the right job for her.

Maybe she wasn't a Professional Student anymore, but she had a job she loved, though she understood the importance of balance and knowing when enough was enough when it came to work. She continued to talk to Julia Steinhert weekly, to stay on top of her stress management techniques and continue to work through some of her troubles regarding hiding information from those outside of the DOL. She was making progress. It was crazy to think that just over a year ago, she had been graduating from NYU, no idea what her future would hold. Not that she had a very clear idea now, but she was definitely more excited about what the world had in store for her.

LONGWOOD PUBLIC LIBRARY
800 Middle Country Road
Middle Island, NY 11953
(631) 924-6400
longwoodlibrary.org

LIBRARY HOURS

Monday-Friday	9:30 a.m. - 9:00 p.m.
Saturday	9:30 a.m. - 5:00 p.m.
Sunday (Sept-June)	1:00 p.m. - 5:00 p.m.